A Vampire in New Hampshire

I glanced around with my Magic Sight to ensure we were alone. If he was part of a pack, then there could be three or more of them around. When my Sight revealed nothing else in the vicinity, I rushed the monster. *If only I had my sword,* I thought as I threw a blast of energy at the monster. It turned its face toward me as the power struck it, sending it flying into a tree.

One myth is that vampires can fly. Nope. It fell with a *thud* to the ground, and for a moment, lay there stunned.

I ran to Oni and examined him. The monster had not bitten him. He was dazed, as though drunk, his head lolling lazily as he tried to focus on me. His eyes kept wandering aimlessly, and his mouth hung slack. He muttered something unintelligible. Vampires can't hypnotize their victims, but they can cause that dazed stupor. It won't last long, but it was usually long enough for the monster to do its worst.

I rose as the vampire stalked toward me. It halted its advance when we were ten feet apart. It sniffed, wrinkling its nose in consternation.

"What are you?" it said through clenched teeth.

"Wouldn't *you* like to know?" I said.

Copyright © 2021 by Brad Younie

First paperback edition: February, 2022

Book design by Brad Younie
Cover Art by Gordon Napier

ISBN 978-1-7333715-6-8 (paperback)
ISBN 978-1-7333715-8-2 (hardback)

01

www.bradyounie.com

A SORCERER'S GUIDE

TO MAGIC,

MONSTERS,

AND THE

MYTHIC WORLD

BRAD YOUNIE

ALSO BY

BRAD YOUNIE

Bad Luck

Chapter One

The circle took up most of the room, its outline marked in chalk upon the hardwood floor. The five points of the star within met the ring to form a complete image. Four candles set along the drawing's edge flickered fitfully, casting an eerie glow about the dim space. Incense hanging thick in the air assaulted my nose as I stood to survey the scene.

Yes. It looked good.

I drew the black hood of my robe over my head, stuffing my ponytail inside, and knelt before the altar. I grasped the hilt of my sword, a noble's rapier from the seventeenth century, and rose, taking a step back. All was ready. The spell-casting could begin.

"Malcus! *Malcus Molova!*" A woman's voice called from downstairs. "Is that incense I smell? You're not doing magic, are you?"

And there it went. Hours of preparation and the ritual was doomed.

"No, Aunt Elise! I'm studying. Incense helps."

"But you haven't started school yet!"

"I'm getting ready!"

I waited in silence, my body tense, listening for the sound of approaching feet.

"Good idea! Your first year at a human school will be hard. But get rid of that incense!"

I sighed. "Yes, Aunt Elise!" At least she didn't try to stop me.

My eyes went to the closed window, then to the edge of circle in which I stood. I couldn't leave the ritual as it was. Too much power had already been invoked. If I stepped across that chalk line, a lot more than my body would cross with it. The magical energy I had pooled up would escape, and without the guidance of my will, who knew what it would do. I had to open a magical door that would let me, and only me, out. With a quick swish of the sword, I created the doorway in the circle and strode through. Climbing onto my bed, I pulled the shade and opened the window. I squinted as the afternoon sunlight flooded my bedroom, ruining the atmosphere of the ritual. The smoke that hung heavy in the air filtered out through the screen to be carried away on an October breeze.

I stared at the three-foot-diameter circle that took up most of the available space. *I need a better magic room*, I thought. Although I'm a sorcerer and can wield the magic within me, a ritual enables me to cast spells that are beyond my current ability.

I reentered the circle through the opening I had created with my sword and sealed it the same way. Any normal person watching me would see me swinging my sword for no reason. But I felt the power flowing around me. Although the magic couldn't escape through the door I had built, it would interfere with the ritual, and thus the spell. So, I swished my rapier like I had before, and mentally removed the portal, leaving nothing but the wall of energy that belonged there. Then I returned to the altar and continued the casting. I stared at the picture of my parents. It was a photo I had taken of them on our trip to Rome. It was been a great trip. My smile vanished as my goal came back to me, and I concentrated on the image. I stretched out my thought, away from my body, outward into the world. They weren't in Rome, as the image showed. I opened my mind and sent out the feelers, looking to catch a nibble from them.

It took forever, and my strength waned, but I kept pressing. They were out there, somewhere, and I needed to find them. But they evaded detection.

The vastness of the world vanished before me, and my smoke-filled bedroom appeared with a suddenness that made me stagger backward in alarm.

"Damn it!" I cursed. "Why didn't it work? It should have worked. I should have found them."

After a minute to regain my composure, I dismantled the circle, packing the photo carefully in my desk drawer.

Exhaustion washed through me, since I had used all my power on a spell that should have taken a fraction of it. I slouched down the stairs and into the kitchen. Aunt Elise was there. She had just pulled a sheet of chocolate chip cookies from the oven.

She nodded a greeting toward me as I grabbed an energy drink from the fridge. "Homemade cookies are perfect after a long casting."

I flashed a surprised glance at her.

She gave me an I'm-no-idiot look, then smiled again.

"You're looking for them." She took a spatula and transferred the cookies to a serving tray. "It only makes sense. Sometimes I wish I could."

Aunt Elise was about as mundane as they come. We both came from a long line of sorcerers, but she never seemed to develop any powers. I had never seen her cast a single spell. Now, that might make sense while hiding here among humans, but not in my parents' home where no one but sorcerers lived. Yet, she never showed any hint of magical ability around me. Still, she was part of the family, she kept our secret. Like all mythic creatures, sorcerers have to keep their identities concealed. We might be part human, but we're still supernatural, and therefore as threatened by humanity as vampires and werewolves.

Humans can be dangerous when they're scared. They hunted trolls to extinction, which was an amazing feat in itself. (Trolls were twenty-foot tall monstrous creatures with a tendency to eat everything that moved). And now, they're nothing but myth and legend. Goblins have endangered status even though humans don't know they exist. Goblins aren't too bright, and their disguises are usually confused with pests. With our magical abilities, sorcerers would probably be next on the extinction list if they knew we weren't human.

Aunt Elise joined me at the table and offered me the tray. I took three cookies and stuffed a whole one in my mouth as she sat down opposite me.

She smiled at me. "You've only been here a few days and you already tried to locate your parents. Marta warned me you were tenacious."

"I couldn't find them," I said, after swallowing.

"Because they don't want to be found. What they're doing

is important and dangerous. They have to stay hidden."

"But why? What are they doing that's so dangerous?"

"You're too young to know."

"I'm fifteen! I'm almost an adult."

Aunt Elise chuckled. "Not quite, dear. You've got a few years to go."

"I can get the information from you."

"I would like to think you wouldn't do that."

Part of me wanted to, but I knew better. You don't invade the minds of people you care for.

"No, I wouldn't."

"That's good. Besides, they never told me, and I didn't want them to. The less I know, the safer I am."

"But it's Alliance work?" I posed it as a question, though I knew the answer.

"The hard jobs always are."

"Sometimes I wish they never joined." My parents worked for The Alliance of Mythical People, or A.M.P. It's a secret organization dedicated to keeping the existence and location of supernatural people and creatures hidden from humans. They travel all over the world on important missions. I was proud of them. But they rarely left me for long. This time they planned to be gone for nearly a year.

Aunt Elise shrugged. "But they *are* in the Alliance, dear. We have to make do. So, I get to visit with my favorite nephew. And you get a break from your magical studies to have a semester in a school with other humans."

"I'm not human."

"You're part human, and that's enough. You're not a monster."

I frowned. "Are fairies monsters?"

"Some are," she muttered. She didn't mean for me to hear, but I couldn't resist my retort.

"And like fairies, some humans are, too."

The breath Aunt Elise released then was something I was getting used to. She tended to do that a lot when we talked. "I stand corrected. It'll still be good to connect with your human side a bit more."

I shrugged. "Whatever. I just want Mom and Dad to come home."

"I know, dear. But you have to stop looking for them. If you find them, you might make it easier for someone else to. And that could put them in danger."

"Okay," I said. She was right, of course. As much as I wanted to search for my parents, it was safer to leave them be.

"Why don't you go wander around? It's nice here, and there's no need to worry about mythical people or creatures. Durbin Point is as mundane a town as you could ask for."

I rose from my seat. "I guess I can study the natives." Armed with a handful of cookies, I went to the door.

"You'll want a jacket!" my aunt called after me.

"I'll be fine!" My words preceded the door as it closed behind me.

A shiver ran through my body. A strong breeze blew down the road from the coast. It tore through my shirt. Another shiver engulfed me, and I rubbed my arms with my hands.

I grimaced as I looked back at the house. I wasn't about to let Aunt Elise think she was right. After a moment's deliberation, I resumed my confident pace down the walkway to the street. I waved my hand in a quick, commanding gesture as I focused on my jacket, which hung on the back of my desk chair. I winced as the sound of a window screen tearing came from the second floor of the house, but then grinned as the coat landed gently over my shoulders. My arms slid into its sleeves, and I left the zipper open as I turned to walk eastward down Dunmore Street toward the seawall.

I'm going to catch hell for that screen, I thought as I embarked on my first solo foray into the human world.

I strolled down Dunmore Street, enjoying the crisp autumn air and observing the neighbors as they busied themselves with their human lives. A few people went from door to car, or car to door. One worked on a boat that sat in his driveway.

Dunmore Street ended at the junction of North Shore Road, which ran parallel to the ocean shore. There, on the far side of the road, the seawall rose four feet from the ground, the concrete structure preventing my view of the ocean from where I walked.

I crossed the street, confident that the vehicles would stop for me. Sure enough, one came screeching to a halt. The car's occupant honked his horn and made rude gestures at me. I smiled and continued across the street. He squealed his tires again after I passed. Humans enjoyed making a big display with their cars. It was a standard show of strength.

The seawall was easy to climb onto. Once there, I took a look around. The ocean stretched out from the edge of the wall to the horizon, with only one small island in sight. I didn't know its name, and nobody lived there. Turning to the north, the wall and its street ran in an imperfect arc, following the shore. Few people walked there, and homes lined the opposite side of the street. To the south looked more promising as the road passed by a small town beach and boardwalk. Many people strolled along the sidewalks, and I could hear their laughter from my vantage a quarter mile distant.

I walked along the seawall, which was at least three feet wide, as I made my way southward toward the hub of activity. The wind whipped around me, causing my jacket to flap and my ponytail to beat against my head and neck. But I enjoyed it. I liked the crisp scent of salty air and the sound of the waves crashing against the wall below. Spray from the ocean sprinkled on my face, but it filled me with exhilaration. I came from Colorado, where there was no ocean, so I reveled in the experience.

I was not alone in my enjoyment of the sea. Couples walking beside the wall often stopped to gaze with longing at the great waves and to point at the boats sailing on the horizon. This became so frequent as I approached the small boardwalk that I jumped down to the sidewalk, lest an onlooker knock me over by accident.

The boardwalk, such that it was, had mostly closed for the season, but a few shops remained open to service the locals. A group of teenage humans congregated outside a video arcade. I had heard of arcades; the places filled with antique game consoles, where each machine ran only one game. And all the games were old and pitifully out-of-date. I found it hard to believe any still existed, but here it stood, and it was open.

My study of the human world would begin with Roger's Arcade. I wanted to know what human teens saw in such a dying custom. The entrance took up most of the arcade's wall, to provide easy access for a swarm of kids. I strode through the group of teens at the entrance, who paused their conversation to watch me as I passed by.

The building was deep and dark, allowing the game machines to bathe the place in flashing lights. The beeps and chirps of a hundred different games permeated the air, and I almost fled from the chaos of it. And there was no need for such a wide entrance. It had likely been decades since this business had last seen a mob. Most of the machines were unoccupied, and I could see only a dozen kids, most of whom huddled around the same few games.

I stood gawking near the entrance, lost in the garish noise and lights, staring at the place in awe. Roger's Arcade both attracted and repelled me.

"You going in, or what?"

I jumped at the sudden invasion of my reverie and noticed that the group of kids that had congregated by the entrance now stood around me. They were all taller than me, and at least a year older. The one who spoke, who I took to be their leader, had broad shoulders and large biceps. He must have been used to hard labor.

"You just going to stand there?" the muscle-bound kid prodded. He looked down at me with a curious expression. I think he was trying to figure me out. Although my plan was only to observe, I knew I had to interact with this group.

"I will, in time. At the moment, I'm looking around." My tone was polite, as my parents had taught me. This was the first time I had ever interacted with humans without my parents to help me. I was alone and didn't feel comfortable with my "people skills."

The leader laughed. "Come on! I'll show you around."

"I don't know you. It's not smart to follow strangers."

Another chuckle. "Fine. I'm Mark, and this is Jake." He motioned to a boy who was almost as tall as him. He had short, black hair and broad shoulders. He grinned at me, but I wasn't convinced he was friendly. "The little guy there is Pete," Mark continued. He motioned toward a shorter and stockier kid with bushy red hair. Pete's smile seemed genuine. "And that's Nate," Mark finished. Nate, a boy with wispy blond hair and a slim, wiry appearance, sneered. Except for Pete, this group didn't fill me with confidence.

The leader laughed. "Now you know us. Let's go! I'll show you some of the best games." He slapped me hard on the back, then gave me a little push into the building. He stepped forward and put his arm roughly around my shoulder as though to show camaraderie. A predator might do the same thing to prevent me from running. But I showed no weakness and thus made poor prey.

The boy and his friends led me deep into the arcade toward an unoccupied section.

"It appears that game is quite fun," I said, pointing to one with a crowd of kids around it.

"Nah! Too many people. The *best* ones are over here."

He led me to a console in a dark corner of the room. It had a fake gun for a controller, and the screen depicted a street scene, probably in Europe somewhere. It had a first-person view, projecting the appearance that we were there.

The leader held out his hand. "Here, give me some coins and I'll show you how to play."

I shrugged. "You should pay for your play. I'll watch."

The older teen turned slowly to face me, a hint of menace in his expression. "Don't get cheap. I'm doing this for *you*."

"You tell him, Mark!" Pete said.

The intentions of the boys came to me in that instance. They were not befriending me. They wanted me to buy them games. He was a predator, after all. A poor one, since he had failed to see my lack of fear.

I flashed Mark a triumphant grin. "I'm afraid I'm far too smart for such a pedestrian ruse. You can pay for your own games. Now, if you'll excuse me..."

"*Pedestrian*?" The smile had faded from Mark's face, which now turned bright red. He grabbed my shirt roughly with his right hand and shoved me toward the entrance. His friends crowded around, blocking my sight of the surrounding arcade.

There was no misunderstanding Mark's behavior. He meant violence, but the owner of the establishment wouldn't allow it, so he was forcing me outside, where his exceptional muscles would be put to the test. I had erred. I had overlooked Mark's obvious behavior and found myself in a dangerous situation. Now I had to find a way out. I could knock them all away from me with one spell, but I needed to hide my powers from humans. Being a monster, of sorts, blending in was essential. I had to find a mundane way out of this predicament, and quickly.

Mark was much stronger than me. In fact, all four of them were more than a match for me if it came to a fist fight. Running was my best option. As we approached the entrance, I tripped intentionally on my foot and fell forward. This forced Mark to let go of me, sending me onto my hands and feet.

I launched myself forward and ran as fast as I could.

I might not be strong in a fight, but I'm light-weight, and that gave me an edge as I sprinted up the road toward home. All four boys ran after me at a good pace. I made as straight a line as I could up the road, dodging people who walked along the boardwalk.

When I left the boardwalk behind, I found my pursuers had made ground on me. I cursed and redoubled my speed, pushing myself harder. My breath came out in quick gasps with every footfall, and sweat poured down my face despite the cold air. The futility of the chase dawned on me as I ran. As wiry as I was, they outmatched me in strength and stamina. Eventually, I would slow down and they wouldn't. I had to use my mind, which I had a clear advantage with. I could turn down a side street and cross lawns, but that would involve acrobatics, and my steps were already slower and heavier. Across the street was the seawall. Nothing there. I could dive over the wall, but the fall would be too much and the water too cold, and there was a good chance they'd be dumb enough to follow me. Yet at least it would get me out of their sight.

That's it!

A car approached, growing larger as it came closer. At the last moment, I swerved and ran across the street barely in time for the car to miss me. The driver honked his horn. But I didn't care. My pursuers had to stop for it, and that gave me a chance. Reaching the sidewalk, I scrambled onto the seawall and looked back at my erstwhile friends. Mark pointed in true brutish fashion, and then they charged. I waved to them, a smug smile playing across my face.

And then I jumped.

Chapter Two

Don't worry. I had no intention of getting wet. I'm a sorcerer, after all, and although I wasn't allowed to perform magic in front of humans, I certainly could do so from behind a seawall. As a result, when the bullies stuck their heads over the edge, they saw nothing but water. Before I leaped, I had created an invisible platform of energy that protruded from the concrete barrier below me. Then I cast an invisibility glamour once I landed on it. The spell wouldn't dupe a mythic person, but these dopes looked right through me as though I weren't there. The looks of utter bewilderment on their faces were precious.

They argued as I waited on my magical ledge. "I watched him jump!" said Nate.

"So did I!" said Pete.

"He can't have just vanished," came Mark's voice, distinctive, with its deep timbre.

Jake shot a nervous look at Mark. "Do you think he went into the water?"

Mark frowned. "Where else could he have gone?"

I was getting bored. I turned around and looked out at the ocean. The sea stretched out before me in its magnificence. Wind whipped through my hair and I smiled despite the dire predicament I was in. I counted three boats sailing out near a small island.

"This is bad," said Pete. "He might have drowned. The water's freezing."

"He knew what he was doing," said Jake.

"We'd see him if he fell in," Mark said. "It's not that deep."

"Hey!" It was Pete. "We'd better go. I don't want to get caught."

Jake looked right at with eyes that saw nothing but the water below. "Should we call 911?"

Mark nodded. "But we'll do it anonymously. Let's go."

One by one, their heads disappeared, and I heard them walking away.

Now I had to climb back onto the seawall. I looked up. The lip was two feet above my head, so I leaped and scrambled for a hold. This took a few tries. I'm athletic, in a wiry and agile sort of way. But I'm not strong, and the concrete was worn and wet. Still, perseverance won out, and I dragged myself up and clambered to safety. The spell I had cast on myself would last a while still, so I lay there, panting and rubbing my invisible arms for some time. Then I made my way casually back to Dunmore Street. Once there, I hid behind a nearby house and became visible once more.

The ordeal left me exhausted, so I returned home and collapsed on my bed. I learned an important lesson that day: don't mock humans. They are proud and prone to violence!

* * *

Monday morning dawned cold and wet, and I dragged myself out of bed to prepare for my first day at a human school. My family lived away from humans, in a home on the edge of wilderness and magically hidden from the populace. I hadn't thought it necessary to learn about them. Our house had no electricity, magic supplying any comforts we couldn't produce through simple means. As a result, I never watched television and only saw a handful of movies on one of our trips into town.

Aunt Elise insisted I ride the bus, to "enhance my study of human culture." I thought it unnecessary. It was the same as riding in a car, which I'd done. A bus couldn't be any different. But she got her way and so I stood on the sidewalk in front of her house waiting for it. The predawn sky cast the street in a gray pallor. Mist blown in from the cool ocean breeze loitered over the ground as I paced on the concrete. Drawing my schedule from my backpack, I ran down the list of classes. It showed Social Studies for First Period. I wasn't sure what that meant, but it sounded useful, since I didn't know how to interact socially with humans. It was in room 221. Aunt Elise said it was on the second floor. The numbering system looked easy enough, so I doubted there would be trouble.

"What am I doing?" I said abruptly. "Mom and Dad are out risking their lives again, and here I am worrying about school!" I shoved my schedule into my bag and paced around on the sidewalk. This kind of work was typical for them. They were field agents for the Alliance, so they're often sent away on missions. But usually, they weren't gone at the same time. And they'd never been gone for months before. I was supposed to live with Aunt Elise for a whole school year. And they didn't expect me to worry? They could be fighting trolls in Norway or going undercover to root out some cabal of rogue sorcerers. Their lives were in danger.

"I should be with them," I said miserably.

The bus appeared at the end of Dunmore Street, so I stopped pacing and tried to bury my stress as I awaited the giant yellow monstrosity that lumbered down the road. It hissed and squealed as it came to a stop before me. The door opened, and I climbed in. The driver, an overweight woman in her forties, motioned down the center aisle. All the first-row seats were open, which surprised me since they were the most convenient. I slid into one and shimmied over to the window.

This was far different from riding in a car. My first concern was that there were no safety belts on the bench seats that were riveted to the floor. It forced the rickety feel of the vehicle into the forefront of my mind. When the bus lurched into motion, I grabbed the railing in front of me and held on tightly. Each bump on the road seemed to cause the vehicle to bounce like a trampoline. The odd thing was that none of the other children looked concerned.

That brought my mind to the second big difference between buses and cars. The other passengers. At least two dozen kids filled the seats by the time I boarded. The shouts, talking, and screams of the students added to the vehicle's rumbling noise to create an atmosphere of chaos I had difficulty dealing with. It reminded me of the arcade, only worse. This was noisier, more cramped, and it jostled me around with every bump and turn. But the bus didn't crash or break down, and I remained in my seat as we made our meandering way to the school.

Nobody shared my seat or tried to talk to me, which made it easier to study bus customs. I learned several of those as I rode to school that day.

One, the troublemakers sat in the back, as it gave them a tactical advantage. They didn't have to watch their backs and had an unrestricted view of everyone. This aided their pastime of shooting spitballs and throwing things.

Two, the kids could be divided into two groups: those who wore headphones, and those who did not. The former kept to themselves and sat in silence, listening to music. The latter huddled in groups or pairs and talked incessantly. Their words didn't reach me, but they laughed a lot, so these were no scholarly conversations.

Three, the bus driver held authority that the passengers respected. Whenever she told someone to face front or stop throwing spitballs at me, they shaped up right away.

The school was an enormous brick building that stretched out in all directions, making it impossible to estimate its exact size. It had two floors, though, and one section rose to a third. The buses lined up before the large main entrance, and the students filed off as soon as their driver opened the door. I was the first to exit the contraption. I had no intention of meeting the troublemakers who had stood up at once to harass the other children.

Room 221 proved more difficult to find than I had imagined. The two-hundred range did indeed mean the second floor, but each was a maze of hallways, and I had to learn the numbering system for each hallway.

I arrived right after the bell rang. The classroom comprised four rows of single-seat desks that all faced the front of the room, where the teacher's larger desk aimed back at the students. A whiteboard dominated the wall behind the teacher. I wished I had one like that. It would help a great deal with ritual creation.

I approached the teacher and handed him the paper that explained who I was. He wrote my name down on what resembled a roster, then told me which seat to take. A single empty desk stood in the row by the windows, near the back. I scanned the students' faces, and I grinned with satisfaction to see none of the ruffians from the arcade. I sat down and withdrew my Social Studies book from my backpack.

My initial definition of this class was wrong. The subject didn't cover how to behave in society. Instead, the teacher focused on a part of world history.

"We have a new student here," Mr. Wyman said. He motioned toward me. "This is Malcus Molova. He'll be joining us for the rest of the year, so please make him feel welcome."

All faces turned to stare at me: some smiling, others indifferent.

"Okay everyone," Mr. Wyman said. "There's no lecture today. Get into your groups and work on your projects."

The students then moved their chairs and desks noisily to form clusters of three or four people each.

The teacher came over to me.

"Malcus, we're learning about civilizations, and the class has formed teams to build hypothetical ones. Let's find one for you."

Mr. Wyman led me to one such group. I selected an unused desk near theirs and pulled it over.

"Malcus will join your team. Show him what you've done

and include him in the work."

Two girls and one boy looked up at me. The girls huddled beside each other while the boy sat across the table from them.

"This is Kathy Wilkins," said the teacher, motioning toward a blonde, blue-eyed girl. Her smile was bright and cheerful, which I returned as best I could.

"And this is Tracy Mann." He gestured to the second girl. Shorter than Kathy and petite, her brown hair cascaded in silky waves to her shoulders. Her bangs hung down to half conceal her dark eyes. Only the slightest hint of a smile tugged at one corner of her mouth.

"And this is Oni Akio." The boy didn't speak. Though short, he still had a few inches on Tracy. He was Asian, and dressed in the T-shirt and jeans that most of the school boys wore. The kid watched me curiously, as though trying to figure me out.

"What's wrong, Oni?" Kathy said. "You never stop talking."

Oni shrugged, but remained quiet. He continued to stare at me.

"Well," said Mr. Wyman. "I'll leave you all to it. Please make him feel welcome, kids." He left to wander the room, checking on each group.

"Where are you from, Malcus?" Kathy asked.

"Colorado," I said.

"Cool!"

"So, we're creating a civilization?" I wanted to avoid questions about my life and my family since I couldn't tell them the truth.

Kathy nodded. "Oni's done most of it. He's good at this stuff. But we're helping."

I looked over the papers that described the culture they

were building.

"It's a primitive civilization," I said, noting the descriptions of stone structures, swords and bows for their soldiers, and a monarchy for a government.

"That's the rules," Kathy said. "Mr. Wyman told us to create an ancient civilization. We have to work out the government, economics, defenses, and so on."

"It looks reasonable. You've got all the basics." I noticed that the features thus far had a masculine tone, focusing on war and weapons, walls, and moats. Most had been written by one person. I glanced at each of their possessions. The handwriting of the words "Social Studies" on Oni's wire-bound notebook matched the text on the paper.

"What parts did you add?" I asked Kathy.

She tilted her head as she looked at me. "What do you mean?"

"Well, you said you helped, but all I see here is stuff Oni created."

"We started on Friday. We haven't gotten far."

"Is it customary for the men to do most of the work, and for the women to help?" Sorcerers never treat women as lesser than men. Some of the most powerful sorcerers I knew were women. But I supposed humans could be primitive in that respect.

"What the hell!" Kathy gasped and glared at me.

I frowned. "I hope I didn't speak out of turn."

"Screw you," Tracy said simply.

Kathy recovered from her shock at hearing my theory. "You think you're so awesome with your big words and weird talk, but you're just a loser!"

Oni remained silent. He continued to look at me, but now his face creased into a frown.

"Come on, Oni. Tracy," Kathy said, turning away from me. "Let's get to work. Malcus can *help* if he wants."

The two girls ignored me for the rest of the class. I realized I had guessed wrongly about the role of women in human society, and that I had made a faux pas. I tried to apologize for my indiscretion, but Kathy wouldn't let me. She cut me off every time I tried to speak, and I ended up sitting there watching them as they worked. Discovering a way to make up for it would be tough, but I had to try. The girls were nice, and I wanted them to like me. I had reservations about Oni, who never spoke to me, but sneaked glances at me whenever he thought I wasn't looking.

With the room numbering system figured out, I had no trouble finding my next class, which was Mathematics. Oni sat nearby. As before, he watched me as I took my seat. In fact, he kept his eyes on me throughout the period. It was disconcerting. *Is this normal behavior for human kids?* I wondered. A quick look around the place showed that everyone else had forgotten about me and focused on their work. I chose not to pay him any mind. He was a strange boy, but harmless. Instead, I focused my attention on the teacher and listened to the lecture. I excelled in math, so I found the rest of the class to be both enjoyable and easy.

Third Period was Composition. The students were in the middle of a big writing assignment. The teacher, Mrs. Pearson, answered questions and helped a few of the students with their papers, then met with me. She gave me a smaller version of the essay since I had less time to complete it. She was fair and intelligent, and I realized I might learn something from her.

Well, what do you know? I said to myself as I sat at my desk and listened to her speak. *This human school might not be a waste of my time after all.*

I had Spanish next, and then lunch in the cafeteria. I knew the rudiments of Spanish already. My parents, being in the Alliance, considered it important to speak as many human languages as possible. I didn't see their viewpoint, since I could easily cast a spell to translate for me. Still, it was nice to take a class they would approve of.

I went in search of Room 147. As I rounded onto a side passage from the main hallway, I tripped and fell face-forward onto the floor. I leaped to my feet and turned to see the cause of my fall.

Mark from Roger's Arcade stood before me. His muscles flexed and a big grin stretched wide across his face.

There was no mistaking his intentions.

"So," the oaf said as he glared at me, menace etched in every line of his brutish face. "Where were we? Oh, yeah . . . *who's pedestrian?*"

I grimaced. Students in the hallway stopped to watch the altercation. By the looks on their faces, they arrived at the same conclusion I had.

"Why do you think I'm pedestrian?" He stepped closer and grabbed my shoulder with his left hand, his vice-like grip sending shards of pain through my body. "Is it because I'm tough?"

My eyes darted around him, searching for a means of escape. None came.

"Well?" He shoved me roughly against a row of lockers,

which rattled throughout the hall. "Answer me!"

"In truth, I didn't expect you to know what pedestrian meant."

The fist connected with my face before I could focus on it. Intense pain washed over me and my knees suddenly felt like jelly. Something with a metallic taste ran from my nose.

I needed to learn to hold my tongue with this rogue.

"Your insistence on violence doesn't help your argument. If you want to be taken seriously, you must—"

I twisted my head in time to avoid a second fist in the nose. Instead, the punch buffeted my cheek and sent me into the lockers again. It's amazing how pain in one part of the body can affect muscles in another; such was the case when my legs weakened and I nearly collapsed. In fact, I would have fallen if he hadn't held me up with his free hand.

Mark raised his fist for a third strike. "You're going to regret you ever met me," he hissed.

Of course, I already did, but I chose not to voice that opinion. I lifted my arm to defend against the next blow.

"Mark Rousseau!" The voice came from the main hall I had so recently left.

My attacker glanced that way and then sighed. He lowered his fist, but kept his hand on my shoulder, holding me in place.

Mrs. Pearson, my Composition teacher, stormed toward us, anger and disapproval twisting her otherwise kind demeanor.

"Mr. Rousseau, you are well aware of our policy about fighting."

"But Mrs. Pearson . . ." the brute whined, as though afraid of the elderly woman who stood before him. "He started it!"

She raised an eyebrow. "He attacked you?"

"He called me *pedestrian*."

Humor twitched on the teacher's face, but she remained stern as she glared at Mark. "There is no fighting in this school. You know this better than anyone. Now, let's go, the both of you."

Mark released my shoulder, and I toppled to the floor.

Mrs. Pearson frowned and helped me up. She fished in the pocket of her sweater and removed a handkerchief, which she placed in my hand. "Pinch your nose—it should stop bleeding."

I took the cloth and wiped the blood from my face, then followed the two along the hall toward the front entrance.

She led us to the main offices, then told us to sit in chairs that lined the wall outside them. With a look of caution at Mark, she disappeared through the door.

I was *thrilled*.

This was clearly an out-of-the-ordinary situation, and I had the opportunity to witness firsthand what happened in a disciplinary case. *They must be gathering a tribunal,* I thought excitedly. Beyond that door was a courtroom of some kind, and I would have to plead my case. I wasn't concerned, since I was an innocent victim, and Mark was apparently a repeat offender. I wondered what kind of sentence Mark would get. He was, after all, a child. I looked at my enemy. He fidgeted nervously, casting dark glances at me. He was worried, but he didn't look like someone in dire straits.

The teacher emerged from the office and strode away down the hall. A woman then called us in. I followed Mark through the door. I wanted the look of guilt on his face to be the first impression the tribunal received upon our arrival.

But there was no tribunal.

We entered a small square room, much smaller than any of my classrooms. The walls were adorned with ordinary things: a bookshelf, a filing cabinet, photographs of someone's children. A big wooden desk filled the far half of the room. The man who sat behind it was middle-aged and mostly bald, what hair he had flecked with gray. A nameplate at the edge of his desk read "Harold Lansing, Vice Principal." There was no vaulted ceiling. No dais. No throne for the judge. And there was certainly no jury.

The man motioned for us to take the two empty chairs before us. Mark obeyed, seating himself and scanning the room nervously, unable to meet the man's eyes.

I frowned and looked around, at a loss.

"Have a seat, Mr. Molova," the man said. His voice was strong and stern. I looked at him with renewed interest. Perhaps this man was the sole bearer of discipline for the school. A man of power whose words must be obeyed at great cost.

With a nod of respect, I lowered myself into the open chair and waited patiently for the proceedings to begin.

"Fighting is not permitted in this school." His gaze went from Mark to me and back to Mark.

My nemesis opened his mouth, but was silenced by a sharp look from the vice principal.

"And we have zero tolerance for bullying."

"I wasn't bullying," Mark said. His voice shook. He was nervous. I had not expected that. This boy was large and strong and assertive. He was behaving meekly, which did not fit his personality.

"That would be a first, Mr. Rousseau. You know what I told

you. One more time and you get suspended."

"But he started it!" Mark exclaimed. "He called me *pedestrian*."

Vice Principal Lansing frowned and turned his gaze on me. "Did you?"

I took a moment to compose my thoughts. It was important that I pled my case carefully, even though I was a faultless victim in this exercise.

"I'm afraid I did, but in my defense, it was yesterday, outside of school, and in response to attempted theft."

"I didn't try to steal anything?" Mark shouted, twisting to glare at me.

"Did you, or did you not, try to coerce money from me?"

"Screw you!"

"Mr. Rousseau," Vice Principal Lansing cut in. "Answer him."

Mark's eyes shot helplessly from the man to me. Then he lowered his head in shame.

"Yes."

"And all he did was call you a name, after you provoked him."

The boy scowled, but looked down at his lap. "Yes."

"And so you hit him, twice, in the face."

Mark closed his eyes, defeated. Then he nodded.

"Mr. Molova," the vice principal said. "Did you punch, or otherwise try to hurt Mr. Rousseau?"

"No, sir. In the strictest sense, I did not participate in the fight."

The vice principal nodded. "You may go now, Malcus. But I'd be more careful with your choice of words in the future. It doesn't pay to insult those who are stronger than you."

I rose. "Thank you, sir. Those are wise words." Then I turned and left the room. I continued to shake, and my legs still felt like rubber, but my nose had stopped bleeding and my strength gradually returned as I walked.

Human high school was far more difficult than I had believed. The thought raced through my mind as I continued to my class. It seemed the most important lessons had nothing to do with the school's curriculum.

Chapter Three

The cafeteria was the first impressive room I encountered at the school. It was wide and deep, with support pillars rising from floor to ceiling at even intervals. The walls were painted in bright blues and yellows. Long, rectangular tables filled nearly every open space in the room, leaving a maze of narrow gaps between them that students traversed with their food. The scene was chaotic. No fewer than a hundred students occupied the room, either seated at tables, standing in line for the kitchen, or simply milling about. And with every kid talking, the sound was deafening. I had to take a deep breath to calm my nerves before entering.

The kitchen had two entrances, one on either side of the room. Students lined up to enter through one doorway while kids holding trays laden with food exited from the other.

I joined the queue and waited as the line inched along. Kids talked to each other, leaving me to my own thoughts. The day was half over, and not only had I failed to make any friends, I had managed to alienate everyone I met. My morale was low when I finally entered the kitchen. The food looked unappealing, and my thoughts drifted to Aunt Elise's meals, which were always delicious. I told myself to bring a lunch to school from that point onward.

When I emerged into the cafeteria, I scanned for a place to sit. The two girls from my Social Studies group sat at a table with two friends, but there were a couple of empty seats. I made my way toward their table, but when Kathy noticed me, she scowled and shook her head.

She was still angry at my error and clearly didn't want an apology. I turned away and sought a seat at the end of a long table that held only two students. They ignored me as they ate and chatted. I listened in, as I was here to study humans, but I could make no sense of their conversation. I was missing much needed context, and they spoke in a dialect I couldn't recognize. The term "OMG" had no meaning for me.

I had only taken three bites of my cheeseburger when a girl took a seat opposite me. She was of average height, but that was her only common feature. Her long, obsidian hair cascaded down her back in gentle waves. A small braid around her head kept her hair from her face. Her fair skin appeared pale compared to the blackness of her hair. Her eyes were large and brown and drew me in with an intelligence I had rarely seen in a human. She had a beautiful smile, and I felt my body react in a way I wasn't used to. It sent heat to my face, which made me uncomfortable.

"I hope you don't mind me sitting here," she said as she set her tray on the table before her. "You were all alone and looked interesting. You must be new here."

"Yes," I said. "I'm Malcus Molova. I moved here from Colorado."

She grinned and my face turned redder. "Hello Malcus Molova from Colorado. I'm Brigid. Brigid Talog."

"That's an unusual name," I said.

"So is Malcus Molova. Both names start with the same letter. They say writers shouldn't make up names like that."

"Mine's not made-up. Where does Talog come from?"

"It's Welsh. Molova . . . that's Russian, isn't it? Or Czech?"

"Romanian."

"Ah." She lifted her burger and bit into it. It was juicy and rare. My own burger was brown and overcooked.

"That's a very red burger. I didn't think they made any like that here." All the patties I saw in the kitchen resembled mine.

Brigid grinned. "They don't. But I know one of the cooks." She gave me a quick wink. I didn't know what that meant, so I ignored it.

"Is this your first day?" Brigid asked after a sip of cola.

I nodded as I ate.

"Must be rough, starting school mid-semester like this."

"It is. I'm having trouble making friends."

"Really? I find that hard to believe. You seem quite friendly to me."

I shrugged. "I tend to say the wrong things."

"Well, you haven't yet with me."

"Give me time. But if I say something insulting, it's unintentional."

"I'll keep that in mind."

We ate in silence for a few awkward minutes. I wanted to talk to this girl, but for the first time, words escaped me. I could think of no way to impress her, save with magic. And that was off-limits.

Brigid motioned off to one side with her head. "That boy is staring at you."

It was Oni. He sat at a table with a few boys. They talked and joked amongst themselves, but Oni kept looking over at our table. I knew he was staring at me because he had been doing so all day. But this presented the opportunity to say something nice to her.

"He's probably staring at you."

She smiled. Point scored. "Nope. I noticed him before I came here. He seems fascinated by you. Do you know him?"

"No. He's in a couple of my classes, but I've never talked to him."

"I wouldn't trust someone like that. His obsession can't be healthy. I'd find out what he's up to, if I were you."

"I might do that," I said. The thought had crossed my mind.

She rose and hefted her backpack, then lifted her empty tray. "I've got to go. I have to talk to a teacher. See you later, Malcus Molova." She walked away through the crowd.

I watched her go, then noticed many other boys eyeing her, too.

There was something about Brigid Talog that was odd, besides her name. My gut told me to be careful of her, but every other part of me hoped to see her again.

Sixth Period brought me to Room 203 for Science. I showed my teacher, Mr. Fahey, the paperwork. He gave me a textbook, then assigned me an empty desk. I watched as more kids filed in. Tracy entered as the bell rang, and she paused when our eyes met. I smiled, trying to appear apologetic. She didn't return it as she took her seat right in front of mine.

I wanted to talk to her, but I was never given the chance. Mr. Fahey began his lecture, which was on biology and cells, and there was no opportunity to talk. When the bell rang at the end of class, Tracy grabbed her books and darted from the room, as though to avoid me.

Did I make her that nervous? I entered the hallway at a more leisurely pace and chose not to chase after her. Perhaps I could apologize the next day in Social Studies.

My final subject was Physical Education, which I discovered most kids called "Gym." This, I learned, was because it was typically held in the school's gymnasium.

"We're playing basketball today," Coach Walker told me as the students warmed up with stretching exercises.

"How do you play?" I asked.

"You don't know how to play basketball?" He looked surprised.

"I'm sorry, no."

"Where have you been all these years, kid?"

"Colorado," I said.

"And they don't have basketball there?"

"I was homeschooled," I replied. Aunt Elise instructed me to say that if my lack of knowledge in human culture caused a problem.

The coach frowned, clearly skeptical, then shrugged. "Well, I'll give you the basics, and then you can figure out the rest as we play." He gave me a rundown on the rules, which seemed easy enough, and then sent me onto the floor.

Brigid stood among the students on the gym floor. She wore black shorts, white sneakers, and a plain blue T-shirt. A group of five boys crowded around her. They fawned over her like dogs begging for food. She was beautiful, but it surprised me to find so many boys vying for her attention when there were other pretty girls in the gym. These other girls clearly shared my opinion as they glared at the spectacle with undisguised enmity.

This increased my sense of Brigid's oddity. Something was definitely off about her. *Could she be a monster?* Many types of monsters can pass for human, either by a spell, like a glamour, or by naturally appearing similar.

I looked at Brigid using my Magic Sight. This is a different way of seeing the world. It's like when you cross your eyes to make everything appear blurry, only I let my eyes tap into the magical energy that's all around us. The Magic Sight lets me see monsters that would otherwise be hidden from me.

Everything dimmed to a dull gray. I could see well enough, but it all seemed drab, with muted color. Each person in the room, however, was bathed in a brilliant gold light. You see, every living thing has magical energy inside it, even if they can't use it. And all magic lights up when using this mode of vision. Everyone appeared about the same. Everyone but Brigid, that is. She glowed brighter than the others, but not too brightly. And her appearance didn't change. If she were a disguised orc or something, she would have looked it to me. So, whatever she might be, her natural form was like a human. Could she be mundane with that much energy? Of course. But when coupled with everything else I saw, I doubted she was. But if she were magical, what was she? A magical human? Was that even possible?

A whistle sounded that yanked me from my reverie. I switched back to regular sight and ran out to join the rest. When Brigid saw me, she beamed and waved. The five boys glared at me darkly.

Great.

The basketball game was frustrating. Although I felt I understood the rules well, I failed to master the concept of "dribbling." Every time I tried, the ball would bounce away from me and the other team would gain control of it. Eventually, my teammates refused to pass it to me.

I stood beside our opponents' net and watched the game as the players stayed on our team's side for most of the game. David Grimes, one of the taller and more skilled students on my team, got hold of the ball and ran, dribbling, down the court in my direction. I studied his technique, but failed to understand how it was different from what I did.

As David swerved to evade an opponent, the ball bounced away from him, rolled past several people, and came right to me. At once, the entire mass of players on the other team ran at me.

My mind raced. I knew I had to keep it from them, so I picked it up. Nobody on my team was within reach to throw to. I looked at the hoop that rose up beside me. I aimed and threw, nearly straight up.

The orange orb flew into the air, then hung seemingly motionless for a painful moment. Then it descended with a *swish* through the net to bounce loudly on the floor.

My opponents all walked away with their heads bowed, while my teammates jumped up and down with excitement.

I grinned. I had finally shown my worth. Of all my immense skills, throwing a ball straight up was the one that gained me fame. It still makes me laugh.

Throughout the rest of the game, I stood in my new position, waiting for the ball to come my way. I wasn't always good at catching it, but when I did, a point was scored. We still lost, but nobody blamed me for it, and I considered that a triumph.

Brigid had another strength. She had a way of distracting the boys so they would miss balls passed to them. However, she never used that trick on me, even though we were on opposite teams. I was unsure if she chose not to, or if she *couldn't*. If it was a magical power, it might not have any effect on a sorcerer. Our natural magical affinity makes us resilient to certain types of spells.

The game ended shortly before the bell rang. I was sweaty and hot, but as this was the final period of the day, I decided not to shower in the locker room. I changed back into my regular clothes and made my way to the front of the building.

The bus ride turned out to be eventful. I took my seat in the front row, like before, and did my best to listen in on the conversations that occurred. At first, they all seemed to be about school projects and what boy liked what girl. But then something grabbed my attention:

"Did you hear about Mark Rousseau?"

"What about him?"

"He got suspended!"

"No way!"

"Way! He was caught fighting. He punched out the new kid. Gave him a bloody nose and everything. A teacher saw it."

"Well, Mark had it coming!"

"I wonder what the kid did to get Mark so mad?"

"He stood up to him."

"Got to be more than that?"

"Mark was teasing some kid and the new kid tripped him."

"Have you met him?"

"I've seen him. He's weird."

"Kathy Wilkins talked to him. She says he's sexist. He thinks girls can't do things by themselves without men."

"Ugh! What a jerk!"

"Still, at least he got rid of Mark."

"I wouldn't want to be him when Mark sees him outside of school."

"Yeah, he'll kill him."

I didn't like the way the conversation turned. With the elation from my success against Mark, it hadn't occurred to me that I might meet him in town. I could be forced to use magic. I did it once without getting caught. With luck, I could do it again.

I also didn't appreciate how the story had changed. I never tripped Mark. Although that part made me look good, the fallacy of it bothered me.

Chapter Four

"How was your day?" Aunt Elise said as we sat down to dinner.

"It was . . . Interesting." My nose looked better although I had a bruise beside it. It hadn't broken and it only hurt a little, as long as I didn't touch it.

"Did you find humans to be more than you expected?"

"I guess you could say that."

"You're being vague. I want details. Tell me what happened."

My sigh came out more like a groan of annoyance. "Well, I got in a fight, I offended a few kids, and I met a girl who might be a monster."

Aunt Elise raised an eyebrow. "Really? All that?" She frowned. "I see the bruise now. I hadn't noticed it before. We'll take care of it after dinner. First, let's discuss the fight. You didn't use magic, did you?"

I flashed her a smug look and pointed at my nose. "Would

I have *this* if I had used magic? Please show me some respect."

She blinked, and her cheery expression faltered. I didn't know why. "It's my job," she said. "But I think I might know the cause of your troubles. Tell me about the fight."

I described the incident, including the events at the arcade that led up to it. I left out the part about using magic. There was no need to upset her.

Aunt Elise considered the story.

"Do you know where you went wrong with this boy?"

I nodded. "I mocked him. That's what caused the trouble. I should have said something like 'Gee, I've got to go now,' and left them there."

She chuckled. "Yes, something like that."

"I heard he might come after me outside of school," I said.

"Yes. And how do you plan to deal with him, should that happen?"

"Run, I suppose. I'm not allowed to use magic, even though my parents do in public all the time." It wasn't fair. I could be as discreet as them.

"It takes experience and maturity to use magic safely in public. You don't have enough of either, but you're getting there. Resisting magic when being chased yesterday was a good step towards that maturity."

I winced in my mind and tried not to let it show on my face.

"If that boy catches you, he will hurt you badly. If you're careful, you can use a simple spell, like a glamour, to elude him. But you must not be seen when you cast it and when you release it. There can be no witnesses."

I was proud that she suggested the same spell I used the

other day. It showed I had the right mindset for spell-casting in public.

"Now, tell me about offending the kids."

Aunt Elise listened to the story, which elicited a sigh and a headshake with eyes closed. When I finished, she smiled. "You're a lot like your mother," she said.

The change in topic surprised me, so I frowned. "How?"

"Marta knew little about human history and culture, too. For a long time, she didn't think it was necessary." Aunt Elise chuckled. "All three of my older sisters didn't. I'm glad she eventually learned the importance of it."

"If none of your siblings cared about human culture, why did you?"

"Our parents saw the troubles my sisters were having. Living in a world dominated by humans meant we should know as much as we could about them. But, by the time our mother realized her mistake, it was too late for my sisters. So, she refused to make the same mistake with me."

"I never knew that. Mom never talked much about her family."

"Marta was always a loner. She was a powerful sorcerer and always looked ahead. She had already left home by the time I was in my teens."

My aunt took a sip of tea. Then she told me how the human children had interpreted my statement. She explained the history and why the girls would be so sensitive. I had no idea that human women had fewer rights than men in the past. All the women I had interacted with were treated as equals, but they were all mythic people. I had lived a secluded life among other sorcerers. I had had no interest in the human world before, even though I grew up on the edge of it. My magical studies consumed most of my attention.

"Now, tell me about this girl," Aunt Elise said, coming to the most important topic last.

I described what I witnessed about Brigid, then summed up the problem. "She had a greater amount of magical energy inside her. I saw it. She had a way of attracting, and distracting, boys. And, well, she just seemed odd."

Aunt Elise smiled during my explanation and then chuckled. "Oh, Malcus. There are some things that all the research in the world can't prepare you for. You will find that even mundane girls might possess powers over you that you could not have predicted."

"Mundane girls can cast spells?" I asked.

"No, no. Nothing like that. The power they wield is mundane, but it can be strong. What you described is a beautiful girl, and beautiful girls can attract and distract boys quite easily. Without magic."

"But there were other pretty girls there, and the boys ignored them."

"This Brigid knows how to handle boys better than other girls. It's a matter of skill, Malcus. She knows how to use her beauty to her advantage. I'd be careful of her. It seems she has an interest in you. You might get caught by her charms. Her non-magical charms," she added quickly when I opened my mouth to protest.

"If you think she's not a monster, then what about the extra energy?"

Aunt Elise considered my question. "Some humans have more than the usual amount of it. I think you should assume she is human until she does something that truly suggests she's a monster."

"Like eating raw meat? I swear, her burger was barely cooked."

"There are humans who like their meat rare. More than you'd think. But if not, then we're talking about either a vampire or a ghoul. Vampires can't survive in daylight, and ghouls . . . well, they would have a harder time passing for human."

"How?" I knew little about ghouls.

"They have certain physical quirks. Their eyes are always bloodshot, and they can go berserk around open wounds, which can be a big problem. They're more monster than mythic, and their behavior goes along with that. And they smell."

"They smell?"

"Like rotten flesh. And it's not only because they eat it. There's something about their physiology that makes it happen."

That certainly did not describe Brigid. "Okay, so she's neither vampire nor ghoul. Does that mean she *can't* be a monster?"

"Of course, she could be a sorcerer. But they emit a *lot* of energy. It would have been obvious with your Magic Sight. There might be other monsters that fit her description, but I'm not an expert. Treat her like a human, but keep your eyes open."

"Thanks, Aunt Elise. I think I learned a lot on my first day of school." I had never put much stock in my aunt because she had no magical talents. But this talk was useful. She showed an understanding of human behavior that I greatly lacked. From this point onward, I would respect her opinions and tell her about my experiences. And tomorrow, I would try to fix the wrongs I had made, and perhaps make some friends.

homework. Thoughts of Brigid stole into my mind and made it hard to focus on my assignments. Could she be a monster like me? If so, it's possible she's not bad. After all, there are plenty of mythic people that aren't evil. I was living proof.

I sat at my bay window and opened it. The cold night wind fluttered the curtains, and I breathed in a great draft of salt air. It helped me think. The streetlights cast a glow in large circles along the road. Windows were lit along the street, and although the occasional car passed by, the scene was quiet and serene.

Brigid was a pretty girl, and she liked me. I needed to find out if she was a monster or an exceptional mundane. Aunt Elise said to assume she's human, but I couldn't do that.

Movement caught my attention as I gazed absently out the window. Something had moved across the street. I strained to see what it was, but in the darkness of early evening, everything was in shadow. *Could someone be over there?*

Mark. The gossip on the bus came back to me. Mark was looking for revenge. A weight settled in my chest at the thought of that tall boy with his big fists. I was safe inside my house, but if he was hanging around waiting to waylay me when I left . . .

Closing my eyes, I took a deep, calming breath. It was only a shadow, a hint of movement. It might not be Mark. It could be anyone, even a dog. I needed to know for sure, to understand my peril.

The light in my room behind me prevented any chance of seeing details. With a wave of my hand and the merest hint of magic, I flipped the switch on the wall across the room. I was plunged into blackness. Then I focused on the shadows.

Something moved by the corner of a house. Using my Magic Sight, the energy of a human body pulsed and throbbed in the spot from where the movement had come. The person was too small to be Mark. It was another kid, probably my age.

I relaxed as understanding sunk in.

The lurker seemed to realize I had noticed him, and ran off down the street, away from the ocean. I knew it was Oni. I wasn't afraid of him, and I was tired of his constant spying. I threw open the ruined window screen and, grabbing my jacket, I climbed onto the porch roof.

Nobody was visible on the street, save for Oni's departing back, so I risked a small amount of magic to glide gently down to the sidewalk. Then I bolted in hot pursuit of my shadow.

The boy led me on a merry chase through my aunt's neighborhood, up one road and down another. But eventually, we reached the outskirts of town, and the forest that surrounded most New Hampshire towns loomed ahead of us. He made for the tree line, hoping to lose me in the woods he was infinitely more familiar with.

His ruse worked.

No more than twenty feet among the boughs, I realized I had not only lost all sign of my quarry but also my way out. I stopped running and, catching my breath, listened for the sound of movement in the trees.

He made a fair amount of racket as he fought his way through the thick foliage since he left the path that was somewhere to our right. I struck out toward the noise, every now and again stopping to reacquire his trail. He had also slowed, finding travel in the forest at night hard.

I switched to Magic Sight, which provided a better image of where I was than the near complete darkness of the woods. Now, I had the advantage. The trail of energy the spy left behind in his mad dash stretched out ahead of me, so I followed it. The hard part was avoiding all the trees. Magic Sight dims everything else, so navigating the woods became even more difficult. I found myself switching back and forth between the modes of vision. I couldn't keep that up forever, though. Even the small amount of power used for the Sight took its toll on my stamina.

Before long, I came to the edge of a clearing. It was about ten feet in rough diameter, and formed a three-way junction of paths, two broad and one narrow. Oni stood in the center of the open area. He leaned forward, his hands on his knees, as he struggled to catch his breath.

I took one step from my hiding place when something big shot past me at an alarming speed from the narrow path into the open. The creature was on top of Oni before I realized what it was.

A vampire huddled over Oni's prostrate form, the boy lying horribly still, as though dead underneath it. In the darkness, they were one shadow on top of another. But I could tell it was a vampire. First, it had almost no magical energy inside it. The inhuman speed and strength were also signs. And, well, it *felt* like one.

I scowled. Oni might have bothered me with his annoying behavior, but he didn't deserve to be vampire food. And did I ever mention *I hate vampires*?

My grandfather, whom I had greatly loved and admired, was killed by a pack of them three years ago. Since then, I had vowed to kill every vampire I encountered, which so far was none. It's not as though they're on every street corner.

And now there was a vampire with its back to me.

I glanced around with my Magic Sight to ensure we were alone. If he was part of a pack, there could be three or more of them around. When my Sight revealed nothing else in the vicinity, I rushed the monster. *If only I had my sword,* I thought as I threw a blast of energy at the monster. It turned its face toward me as the power struck it, sending it flying into a tree.

One myth is that vampires can fly. Nope. It fell with a *thud* to the ground and, for a moment, lay there stunned.

I ran to Oni and examined him. The monster had not bitten him. He was dazed, as though drunk, his head lolling lazily as he tried to focus on me. His eyes wandered aimlessly, and his mouth hung slack. He muttered something unintelligible. Vampires can't hypnotize their victims, but they can cause a stupor. It wouldn't last long, but usually long enough for the monster to do its worst.

I rose as the vampire stalked toward me. It halted its advance when we were ten feet apart. It sniffed, wrinkling its nose in consternation.

Vampires resemble humans, of course, since they're related to them. But their faces undergo a small transformation when they're hungry. Their lips get dry and thin and peel back to expose their teeth, which included the iconic pin-like fangs for sucking blood. Their eyes turn bloodshot. And their noses turn stubby and bat-like. This is likely how the myth of vampires becoming bats came to be. Someone probably witnessed this transformation and lived to tell about it.

This one looked like a man in his mid-twenties, with long,

greasy black hair that hung in lank strands around his pale face. His clothes were wrinkled and dirty. He'd worn them for a while. Weeks, at least. This vamp was a mess.

And it stood several paces from me and stared.

"What are you?" it said through clenched teeth.

I needed a stake. Something sharp to run through its heart. You see, vampires are never good, they don't sparkle, and they definitely don't date humans. They might sometimes "play" with their food. But ultimately, if a vampire sets its sights on a human, it's to kill. That or to turn its victim into a slave, a junkie that's fed enough of the vamp's blood that he can't stand to be without it.

"Wouldn't *you* like to know?" I said. Mocking again, I know, but it was going to attack anyway, and I needed to distract it while I searched for a likely weapon. I scanned the area for something suitable. Trees, trees, and nothing but trees surrounded us. And there were no fallen branches strong enough or pointy enough to do the job.

"You're not human. But are you tasty?" It walked sideways, trying to circle around me, its eyes darting as it looked for an opportunity to attack.

"I'm problematic," I said carefully, keeping my attention on it even as I continued my search. "You can't daze me, and my blood might burn you to a crisp." It couldn't, of course, but it didn't know that.

It lunged at me, launching through the air at a remarkable speed. Although unable to fly, it could leap with tremendous ease and range.

I tried to dodge by diving to one side, but it was far too fast. The monster struck me as I made to move, and the two of us flew backward, my feet leaving the ground with the impact.

My back slammed into a tree. Pain engulfed me, and I nearly lost consciousness. I was momentarily stunned. My vision blurred as the vampire landed easily on its feet before me. Its hands shoved me roughly against the trunk, pinning my arms so I couldn't move. As the scene became clear, I saw the creature inches from my face. Its pale skin looked dry, like a carcass. Its colorless lips were drawn away to reveal yellow teeth and those two fangs. The breath that hissed out in ragged gasps reeked of death. The monster opened its mouth impossibly wide to take its bite, joints in its jaw popping as it did so.

For the first time today, luck was on my side. The tree he held me against was not one of the many conifers found throughout New Hampshire. It wasn't as dense, and it had a lot of long, thin branches.

With all my magical strength, I channeled the tree, becoming as though one with it. The life force of the enormous plant joined with mine and since it had no will of its own, I took full control.

I now wielded dozens of arms, and I sent no fewer than fifteen at my opponent. The branches wound about its arms and legs, and three wrapped about its neck. The vampire struggled to bring its head closer, but my new arms were too much for it. I lifted the pathetic creature off the ground, and I laughed as more of my new wooden limbs grabbed at the monster, whose blood-red eyes grew wide with terror.

In a sudden burst of power, I yanked all the branches back away from the creature, pulling its body with them. Twenty wooden arms yanked hard at the vampire to the right, while twenty more tugged to the left. There was an agonizing moment of hesitation filled only by the creaking of breaking branches and bones. The monster screamed in agony . . . and then *pop!*

The vampire's body exploded in a shower of gore, its four limbs and head being all that was left of the erstwhile monster.

I released control of the tree and its life force separated from my own. When it did, I fell to the ground, and darkness enveloped me.

Chapter Five

I opened my eyes as water splashed on me.

"What the..."

Oni's face appeared above my own, his expression grim.

"Are you okay?" he asked in a near whisper.

I gulped air as I tried to build enough strength to talk. "Exhausted" was all I could muster.

"We have to get out of here. There might be more of them."

"My phone," I said.

He searched my pockets, then stuffed the thin rectangle into my hand, closing my fingers around its edges. I dialed Aunt Elise.

"Malcus?" came her voice out of the speaker. "Where are you?"

"Vampire. I'm exhausted." I handed the phone to Oni. "Give directions." My words burst out in gasps.

As Oni explained, I grabbed the bottle of water he had splashed on my face and gulped down the rest of it.

"She's coming."

I rose to my feet, with Oni's help, and together we made our way down the trail. We trudged along in silence, listening intently for sounds of footsteps. After about ten minutes of slow walking, we heard the sound we feared. Someone—or *something*—ran toward us from further down the path.

Without hesitation, Oni leaned me against a tree and took a Karate stance. I lacked the strength to tell him that fighting was useless. The vampire would daze him again.

The footfalls came closer, *thump, thump, thump, thump*. I tried my best to draw power from the tree, but it refused to respond. I was too tired.

A figure appeared ahead of us, first as a shadow, but details formed as the moonlight filtering through the canopy enveloped it. Blonde hair tied in a bun, a blue jacket over pajamas. Aunt Elise came to a stop when she saw us. With only a glance at Oni, she ran to me, her face twisted in concern.

Oni let his guard down, then looked around nervously.

"Are you all right, dear?" My guardian felt my cheek and forehead with the back of her hand.

My fatigue was so intense, I could barely speak. "Used—all—energy. Dead tired."

"Don't use that word." She motioned for Oni to help, and the two lifted me off the tree. We continued in silence—once again putting our efforts into listening for approaching feet.

We emerged from the trail several minutes later near where her blue Toyota Camry was parked awkwardly on the side of the road. They helped me into the back seat, and Oni climbed in with me as Aunt Elise started the engine.

She said nothing during the drive. My power had been returning slowly during our journey in the woods. It was as though everything I touched gave a little of itself to me as I walked, seeping into my feet with each step and spreading a hint of warmth up my legs. As we rode, the world continued to feed me the magical energy I craved with each draft of air and from the two people near me. First, my breathing grew stronger, then I stopped shaking. My arms, which had felt like rubber only minutes ago, now were stiff, their muscles tingling. I stretched them as best I could in the small cabin.

We pulled into the driveway, and I climbed out. Aunt Elise rushed to my side, and the two insisted on helping me up the front steps, even though I assured them I was all right. Aunt Elise sat me on her living room recliner before bustling to the kitchen to bring cookies and an energy drink. Oni watched me from the couch, his creepy stare from earlier today replaced with concern.

"Why were you spying on me?" I asked Oni.

"I saw you disappear. When Rousseau and his buddies were after you. You jumped off the seawall and vanished into thin air. I wanted to learn more about you." He winced and shrugged. "I guess I got obsessed. Sorry."

I glanced at the kitchen. Aunt Elise hadn't heard. I sighed. "How did you see me? I was on the other side of the wall."

"I was on the stairs. There's a set of them that lets you down to the beach during low tide. I like to go down there and watch the fish."

My eyes closed as sunderstanding hit me. I wasn't careful enough. Maybe it was harder than I thought to use magic in public.

"Okay," I said in a quiet voice. "But let's not talk about it here. I don't want *her* to know." I motioned toward the kitchen with my head.

Oni nodded.

"Thanks for saving my life," he said as Aunt Elise entered the room with the food. I devoured two cookies before the plate touched the coffee table. They did help me recover my energy after casting spells. She was a great cook.

"Did you even know you were in danger?" I asked and washed the cookies down with a gulp of energy drink. "The vampire dazed you right away."

"Yeah, what was that? I was standing there, catching my breath, and then I got knocked over. I took one look at the thing and I suddenly felt out of it, like I was drugged or something. I couldn't concentrate on anything."

"That was the vamp," I said.

"They can't hypnotize, like in the movies," Aunt Elise continued for me as she put more cookies in my hand. "But they can *daze* you, as we call it. You're lucky Malcus was there."

Oni nodded his understanding. "Well, anyway, I remembered everything once it wore off. I remember the fangs, and the smell of death on its breath." He shivered. "If you hadn't killed it, I'd be dead now."

"Or worse," I added. His eyes went a little wide.

"Malcus," Aunt Elise said, her tone serious, businesslike. "Are you certain it's dead? Vampires are resilient. Did you stake its heart?"

Oni laughed. "Oh, yeah! It's in tiny pieces all over the woods."

Aunt Elise frowned. "What do you mean? What did you do?"

I described the fight. She might be a sorcerer by blood, but she can't do magic, so she didn't understand the extent of our powers.

"It might sound extreme, but it was all the situation presented me with."

Aunt Elise leaned back in her chair and considered me for some time. "I would never have believed you could do that. But it explains why you're so tired."

She sighed. "Now we need to find out if there are more of them. Oni, did you recognize this vampire? They look like normal people when they're not hunting."

Oni shook his head. "I've never seen him before. What are vampires like, anyway? Are they like the legends? And what are you people? You're not vampires. But Malcus did . . . I mean . . . that was magic, right?"

Aunt Elise sighed. "Oni, I'm terribly sorry that you had to discover so much about the mythical world. We work hard to keep it hidden from humans, and it usually works out for the best that way. I wish we could erase your memories and let you live here without fear. But I'm afraid those spells are outside our ability." My aunt underestimated my skills, but in this case, she was right. Memory modification is exceptionally complex.

She paused before continuing. "We are a type of people called sorcerers. We're not human, although we're related to you."

"You mean, like Neanderthals? Only not primitive, of course," Oni added right away.

"Something like that," my aunt said. "We call all species of intelligent creatures that are not human 'mythic people.' We try to keep our existence a secret because your kind doesn't react well to us. Most want to live quiet, peaceful lives, and those that don't—well, we're better suited to handle them. Malcus and I are good people. We might be sorcerers and can do some incredible things, but we never use them to hurt humans, or to bring attention to ourselves."

Oni looked from Aunt Elise and then to me, his expression one of awe.

"You're like superheroes. And this is your disguise. This is your Bruce Wayne," he said, looking at me.

I shrugged. "I'll take your word for it." The term "superheroes" was familiar, but I didn't know what it meant. "Who's Bruce Wayne?"

Oni chuckled. "You're kidding, right? Bruce Wayne? Batman? From comic books and movies."

"Oh!" I knew what comic books were. "I don't read them, and I haven't watched many movies."

Oni frowned. "But you live here . . . in *our* world. How can you live with us and not see any movies?"

"I don't live among humans. My home in Colorado is in the wilderness. We come into town once in a while, but only for necessities. Less chance of being found out if we keep away."

"But I live with humans," Aunt Elise said with a light chuckle. "And I have seen plenty of films. And I know Batman. We don't fight crime, but we do our part to keep humans safe and ignorant of mythic beings."

Oni paused and considered his next question. "Okay, so what about vampires? Do I have to worry about them during the day?"

"No," I said. "They burn up in sunlight, like in the legends. But the myths don't get it all right. Most of them sleep during the day since they can't do much in daylight, but they don't have to. They can wake up and fight if disturbed, since their beds are in dark hiding places. They exist on human blood, but they often eat the meat as well. Vampires can gain sustenance from the blood of animals, but not as much. It's like a bad diet. They get a little from it, but not enough to be strong and healthy. So, *every* vampire eats humans. They won't try to be good and can never date a human. It's like kissing a slice of cooked bacon. It smells so good, and tastes so nice, you won't be able to resist eating it for long."

The boy considered that for a moment. "How do you kill them, other than ripping them apart with a tree?"

I laughed. "A stake through the heart is always good, but I'd cut its head off afterward, to be sure. Aunt Elise said they're resilient, and that's no understatement. They're mythical people, so they have magical abilities, only limited in their case. Enhanced healing is their biggest one. Dazing their victims is another. Truly destroying the heart when you stake it would be enough. The biggest myth is that they're undead. They're not. They're living and breathing people. Just extremely hard to kill."

"You could also burn it," Aunt Elise added. "Fire kills vampires as easily as it kills humans. But throwing a candle at one won't make it burst into flames, like in the movies. They're not more susceptible to flame than we are. The only exception is direct sunlight. They're hyper-sensitive to it, and we don't understand why."

Oni was frowning when Elise finished speaking, so the two of us gave him a minute to collect his thoughts. "So, they're alive and intelligent, like we are."

I nodded.

"Then, isn't it wrong to kill them like they're monsters?"

"They *are* monsters," I replied.

"You made a good point, Oni," said Elise, and her tone was far more sympathetic than mine had been. "Ordinarily, I would say that they should be treated like the rest of us, with rights and all that. And there are a few who have come forward and made themselves known to us and worked out an agreeable way to exist without being killers. But that's exceedingly rare, and they're still under constant supervision. The truth is, nearly every vampire is a predator who can't resist killing innocent people. That's why we kill them."

"Okay," he said. "I think that makes sense."

"Good," I said. "Do you have any more questions?"

"A ton, but I won't ask them all. Is it true that they can't enter a person's house without being invited?"

I laughed. "That's all bull. They can break into a house like anyone else can. Although, they usually won't because they don't want to draw attention to themselves. They go for strays, people walking alone in some remote place. Like tonight."

I took another gulp of energy drink. "There's your lesson on vampires," I said. "The important thing is to stay inside at night, or at least in brightly lit public places with lots of people around."

"I'll drive you home, Oni. I think your parents will worry."

"Okay," Oni said as he rose.

"And please don't tell anyone about us or the vampires. We don't need that kind of attention."

Oni chuckled. "Like anyone would believe me."

He paused at the door, his brow creased in thought. "That comment you made in class. You didn't mean that, right?"

I cringed and then forced a pained grin. "I had hoped humans treated women as equals, but I had no idea. I was only trying to understand your culture."

He grinned. "Wow! You've got a lot to learn. So," he said, changing topics quickly. "Are we friends now?"

I raised an eyebrow. "Do you want to be?"

He nodded slowly. "Yeah. I think I do."

"Then, okay. We're friends."

Oni waved to me as he went out the door. "Great! See you at school tomorrow."

I yawned as I stood on the sidewalk awaiting the bus. Once again, the air was cold and mist hung on the ground. But this time, the scene took on a sinister appearance as I glanced nervously up and down the road for vampires. It was near dawn, but the sky was still semi-dark, and a determined vampire with shelter nearby could attack. If that monster had been part of a pack and one of them had witnessed the fight, I would be a target.

Aunt Elise had first suggested I stay home after my ordeal, but I refused. Vampires didn't come out during the day, and I was anxious to repair the damage I had caused with Kathy and Tracy. She then offered to drive me to school, but I turned that down, too. I needed to blend in with the locals, and this was part of the experience. She compromised by watching me from the window as I paced on the concrete.

She had tried to contact other members of our family, but they were all abroad doing work for the Alliance. Knowing few other mythic people, Aunt Elise was unable to get help. We were on our own in this situation. She said we would discuss it after school.

The bus rolled to a stop in front of the house and I boarded. Taking my seat in the front row, I tried to listen in on conversations, but found myself dozing off, my head resting on the window beside me.

I had stayed up late working on a charm for Oni. A vampire had targeted him, and although his attacker was gone, others might try where it had failed. The charm wasn't a proof against vampires, but it would render him immune to the daze the monsters cause in their victims. A vampire trying to take Oni would be in for a surprise when the boy fought back. He would still be woefully overpowered, but it was better than nothing.

I approached my group's table in Social Studies with trepidation. I knew Oni would be friendly toward me after last night, but the girls were bound to still be angry.

"Hey Malcus," Oni said in greeting as I took my seat and set down my bag.

I smiled and nodded, then faced first Kathy and then Tracy, my expression as apologetic as possible.

Kathy smiled at me, while Tracy's face remained deadpan. She, at least, didn't scowl like yesterday. Their behavior was unexpected and confusing, but I decided to forge ahead with my apology nonetheless.

"I'm sorry for what I said yesterday. I honestly didn't mean it the way it came out. I was only trying to say—"

"It's okay," Kathy said, cutting me off. "We didn't realize your situation. It makes sense that you said what you did. You didn't know better."

The look on my face must have been comical because Kathy laughed lightly.

"What are you talking about?" I said, flummoxed. "What didn't you realize?"

"That you're from Romania," Kathy said. "You don't know all our customs. Of course you might think that way."

"But I—"

"Sorry, Malcus," Oni cut me off, a big smile on his face. "I know you had a whole apology ready and all, but I couldn't resist telling them. I told them what you told me."

He winked at me, then, and realization struck me like a slap in the face. Oni had taken it upon himself to smooth things over between me and the two girls. He lied to them, but in this situation, the lie had done more good than bad. I decided to go along with the ruse. It was to my benefit, and revealing the falsehood would put my new friend in bad standing with them.

And to be honest, it would not be difficult to pretend to be a foreigner.

Kathy flooded me with questions about Romania, and Oni flashed me a sympathetic look, clearly hoping I could keep up the lie. Although I had never lived in Romania, my parents had taken me there many times, and so I felt more knowledgeable about that country than the United States, where I grew up. I told them about the countryside, the climate, and the castles, but tried to avoid discussing the people and customs. This wasn't hard, since the mention of castles caught her interest.

"Malcus?" Kathy said, her eyes twinkling at me. "Where's your accent?"

The grin that had been playing across my face during her excited questioning dropped instantly. "What accent?"

"You're *Romanian* accent," she said.

I shrugged. "I suppose I lost it during my years in Colorado. We didn't get out much, but being around Americans probably helped." It wasn't technically a lie. I was born in Romania—Oni's guess was a lucky one—but I had spent nearly all my life in Colorado. I doubt I ever had an accent, but if I had, would I remember it?

Kathy pouted. "That's a shame. I bet it sounded nice!"

"Is it true you got Mark Rousseau suspended?" Tracy said, attempting to change the subject. She had seemed bored by the topic of my alleged homeland.

"Yes, although it wasn't intentional. He confronted me in the hallway, and punched me in the face." Kathy gasped at this. "He got caught."

"And they suspended him, just like that?" Kathy said.

I shrugged. "Apparently, this wasn't his first offense."

"He deserved it," Tracy said. The girl affected an emotionless tone every time she spoke, and almost never smiled. I found her fascinating. That a girl so quiet and serious could be friends with someone so extroverted confounded me. I felt I could learn much from their friendship alone.

"Well, intentional or not," Kathy said. "Everyone's going to know who you are."

I frowned. "I don't know if that's good or bad."

Kathy laughed. "You'll be *famous*. Fame is always good."

Tracy sighed. "Except to Mark's friends. And anyone who thinks you're a snitch."

"A snitch?"

It was Oni's turn to laugh. "A tattle-tale. Someone who tells on people when they do wrong."

"And that's bad?"

"Some people think so. It means they can't trust you if they do something private."

"Ah," I said. "I understand now. But I would think that if my actions were just, they would not hold them against me."

"Oh, I'm sure they're all glad you got Mark suspended. But some people still won't trust you. If you ratted out Mark, who knows who else you'll rat on?"

"That's ridiculous."

Oni nodded. "Maybe so, but that's the way it is."

"But you all trust me?" For some reason, I needed to hear them say they would.

"Of course!" Oni said. "We're friends now."

I looked first at one girl and then the other.

"Duh!" Kathy said, and when I flashed her a confused look, she laughed. "Yes, I trust you. You did all of us a favor, and like you said, you didn't really mean to get him in trouble."

"He did *that* to himself," Tracy added.

I sighed. "I'm glad. I like all of you. I want to be friends."

Tracy nodded her head right away and even leaked the hint of a smile.

Kathy slapped the table with her typical cheery grin. "Well, now that's settled, where were we on the project?"

Chapter Six

Oni joined me as soon as I took my seat in the cafeteria. I had brought lunch with me, but he bought his. Thanks to Aunt Elise, my food looked infinitely more inviting.

"Sorry about the surprise in Social Studies. They were complaining about you, and I didn't like it. So, I fixed it. I would have warned you if I could, but I don't have your cell number."

"We can mend that." I pulled out my phone. My parents had bought me a cell phone before they left. I could communicate with the them telepathically, so I never needed one. Now, they were too far away to reach and in hiding. Still, they felt it would be useful to have while staying with Aunt Elise. I could talk to her while fitting in with human society. With the help of Oni's considerable phone knowledge, we exchanged contacts. I hadn't had my phone long, and it confused me. Computers and I did not get along.

"I appreciate what you did in class," I said. "I didn't know what to say to change their opinion of me."

"Hey, it's the least I could do, considering you saved my life."

"You don't owe me. I hate vampires, so I would have attacked it no matter who it jumped."

"Even Mark?" Oni grinned and shoveled a forkful of some white goop that smelled vaguely of potatoes into his mouth.

I chuckled. "Even Mark. He's a scoundrel, but he deserves to live. Vampires killed a relative of mine. And they didn't *just* kill him. They tore him apart, while he was alive."

"That explains the hostility. But dude, a *scoundrel?* You've got to learn to talk like us—wait! Better yet, keep talking like that. The more outlandish you sound, the more people will forgive your social problems."

I frowned. "Am I really that bad?"

"You called all Americans sexist. But the naïve foreigner line will cover for you."

"Still, I'll try to improve my social skills."

We ate in silence for a few minutes.

"Tell me about you," Oni said. "You're a wizard, right?" He washed his food down with a pint carton of milk.

"I'm a sorcerer. Wizards exist, but they are exceedingly rare."

"What's the difference?"

"Sorcerers aren't human. We're related to humans in some way, but different. And we can control the mystical energies of the world and use them for our purposes."

I took a bite of leftover lasagna and savored it. When I finished, I dabbed my mouth with a napkin before continuing.

"Wizards are humans. They don't have built-in magical abilities, but instead use rituals, talismans, and other tools to help them perform magic. Most wizards are pretty weak."

"You're saying you're not human. You *look* human."

"We do. But trust me, if a doctor cut me open, he'd be in for a big surprise."

Oni's eyes went wide. "What do you mean? You've got two hearts, or green blood, or something?"

"No, nothing like that! In truth, I don't know the details. But my dad told me that our physiology is different on the inside. I think I might have organs you don't. And, well, our magic might go haywire if I was cut open that much."

"Cool!" Oni stabbed a piece of unidentifiable meat and put it in his mouth. He chewed hard on it for a minute, fighting with the gristle. He seemed to want to say something, so I waited patiently for him to finish.

"Now," he said after another gulp of milk. "Are there other mythical beings around here? Like, I had never seen a real vampire before—hell, I never thought they existed."

"There are mythic people all over the world of varying species. But they're good at hiding, and we help them. I'm afraid humans would hunt us to extinction if they knew about us."

"I doubt that."

"Remember trolls? That's what happens to the species that *can't* hide. People like you might accept us, but those in charge wouldn't. They would fear us, and that fear would turn to violence."

"Trolls are myths, right?"

"Why do you think we're called *mythic people*? Yes, they are myths now, but they were once alive."

"Still, trolls were ginormous, and they smashed buildings

and killed everyone. That's way different from a sorcerer."

"Are you saying your government wouldn't be concerned about a person who could do what I did last night?"

Oni cringed. "Yeah, I guess you're right."

"Hello, boys!"

Brigid took a seat next to Oni and smiled warmly at me. Oni's eyes went wide, and he babbled out an awkward "hello." He continued to stare at Brigid as she ignored him and focused on me.

"I hear you're the local hero. Did you really get Mark Rousseau suspended?"

I nodded with a mouthful of lasagna.

"That was kind of dumb, don't you think?" Her lip tugged a wry, playful grin. "I mean, he's tough and now he's mad. He won't leave you alone just because he's not in school."

I washed the food down with water. "I didn't do anything. He punched me and Mrs. Pearson saw it. I got him suspended by being a target."

"Ah, that's more like it. But I still don't like the thought of your handsome face getting damaged by that kid's fists."

"Neither do I, but I'm not certain I can avoid that."

Oni slapped his face with the palm of his hand. The boy was an enigma.

"Well, I'm sure you'll do fine." She gave me a strange face, as if she suspected something. I had barely used magic since coming to Durbin Point, so it wasn't that.

Oni flashed me a look as well, but this one was harder to understand. He smiled, then made his eyes wide as he nudged his head in Brigid's direction. My friend was clearly trying to tell me something about Brigid without her noticing, but I didn't know what.

I gazed confusedly at Oni, which made Brigid glance at him. He covered quickly and shrugged with a goofy grin.

My friend rose and threw his bag over his shoulder. With tray in hand, he cleared his throat. "I have to go. But don't let me interrupt. I'm sure you two have a lot to talk about." He raised his eyebrows in my direction, again trying to send another cryptic message.

He walked off across the cafeteria floor, laughing all the way.

Brigid returned her attention to me, a curious smirk playing across her face.

"I find it interesting that your one friend is the same boy that's been stalking you. There's a story there, somewhere. Care to entertain me?"

I hesitated. I wasn't prepared to discuss how I came to befriend Oni. It would require a lie, and the two of us should devise it to keep it straight. Redirection seemed the appropriate response.

"Oh, he's not my only friend. There are two girls in Social Studies—"

"Two girls? On your second day of school? Well, I have my work cut out for me."

"And what work might that be?" I didn't trust her, so I wasn't about to let her get away with such vague statements.

She scrutinized my face through narrowed eyes, her expression always playful.

"Hmm," she said.

The directness of her gaze, coupled with that inscrutable smile, filled me with a longing to get to know her. To spend more time with her. *It would be nice to see her more often, outside of school.* An idea struck me.

"Brigid, would you be interested in going out with me? Perhaps on Saturday?"

She sighed with satisfaction. "Well, I must admit, I never thought you'd get around to it. But, yes, I'd love to go out with you on Saturday. Do you have a time in mind?"

"I was thinking noon. We could go somewhere nice for lunch, then take a long walk."

She considered my proposal for a moment, and by the slight wrinkle of her brow, she didn't like it.

"Let's make it seven. We could go somewhere nice for dinner, then take our walk. Sound good?"

Why does she want an evening date? Daytime should have been fine. And after last night, I was not inclined to go out after dark. Still, if we kept to public places, it might be safe enough. And it would offer a chance to search for more vampires.

"Of course!" I said at last. "Seven it is." We exchanged phone numbers at that point, and she told me to text her with the details.

We went our separate ways as the lunch period came to an end. I entered my next class in an exceptionally good mood. The upcoming date kept running through my mind, making it hard to focus. I had never considered spending time with a girl before, and now it was all I could think of. Could Aunt Elise be right about mundane girl magic?

I stopped in the foyer after taking only two steps into the house. Something wasn't right. My head cocked slightly as I strained to hear anything out of the ordinary.

It wasn't a sound that bothered me. It was a scent. Or rather, it was the lack of one. Aunt Elise loved to cook. Every morning, she served a freshly cooked breakfast. Every meal was not only delicious, but it was a big process that she reveled in. There was always some kind of home-cooked snack when I returned from school.

Yet today, the house was nearly devoid of sweet scents. She had not cooked all day since breakfast. That was unlike her.

"Aunt Elise!" I called as I entered the kitchen with slow, deliberate steps. The baseboard radiator ticked rhythmically. A motor hummed in the refrigerator. But I heard no sound of movement. I put the kettle on for tea—tea helps clear the mind when spell-casting—and took a handful of homemade cookies. These came from a jar shaped like a furry blue monster with a big, toothless mouth and googly eyes. I always found it ridiculous, but Aunt Elise said it was a famous fictional character. But they were *yesterday's* cookies. Not fresh.

Snack in hand, I mounted the stairs to the second floor. Her bedroom door was open, but I knocked on it, anyway.

"Aunt Elise? Are you in there?"

There was no response. Frowning, I peeked in. Her room appeared like most of the mundane bedrooms I had seen in photographs. Not a single magical artifact adorned her dresser, or sat on her nightstand, or hung on her walls. I supposed it was all a part of the act, but I saw no need to keep up the appearance in her bedroom. After all, she had no reason to let a human in there. There was also no sign of recent use. Her bed was made, and everything seemed in place.

I padded down the hallway, each step barely a whisper on the carpeted floor. The bathroom was unoccupied, and she was likewise not in my bedroom. I left my backpack there as I continued my search of the house. My final stop was a guest room, which was neat and orderly—and vacant.

I returned to the first floor and made a cautious tour there, then descended to the basement. A large open area with wall-to-wall carpeting stretched out before me. Aunt Elise used it as an exercise room while I practiced my fencing. All was now quiet and still. I walked through the open space to the door in the far wall. It led to a small utility room that contained the furnace, hot water heater, and other devices required for the building's operation. It was dark, but it took little effort to tell she wasn't there, either.

My heart raced as my concern for my aunt's safety rose. She wouldn't have left the house unlocked. And with my recent discovery of vampires, I feared the worst.

Once again on the first floor, I entered the kitchen to attempt a telepathic link with her, when I stopped dead in my tracks.

Aunt Elise stood by the stove, pouring hot water from the kettle into two teacups. She looked up and smiled genially at my dumb stare.

"There you are," she said. "I was wondering where you got to."

"Where *I* got to? Where were *you*? I've been looking all over."

"Oh, I've been here all along."

"No you haven't. I searched the entire house—which was empty."

She chuckled as she handed me my cup, then sauntered into the living room. Her feet were bare, which was normal for her, as were her navy blue sweats and gray T-shirt. I followed, my brow furrowed in confusion and frustration.

Aunt Elise settled into a soft armchair and took a sip of tea. She motioned for me to sit. I lowered myself to a corner of the couch.

"I was talking to people and wanted my privacy. I have a hidden room for that."

A hidden room. That would explain the lack of artifacts in her bedroom. Having little magical ability, she would need artifacts to cast even the most rudimentary spells.

"Who were you talking to?"

"The Alliance."

I sat up straight. "About Mom and Dad?"

Aunt Elise shook her head. "I'm sorry, no. About the vampire. I asked for help. All they gave was advice."

"What kind of advice?"

"They said we should find out if there's a pack and destroy it, if there is. Not advice . . . more like *instructions*. They've charged me with controlling the vampire situation in Durbin Point."

"But you don't work for the Alliance," I said.

"Yes I do. I live here on their orders. They wanted me to observe humans and learn their customs. It doesn't pay to be ignorant in the ways of such a large and dominant people."

"Do you think you can destroy a pack of vampires?" I asked, knowing the answer.

She laughed, but there was no mirth in it. "Are you kidding? I'm not a fighter. I doubt I could take on *one* vampire, much less a pack."

"And they won't help?"

Aunt Elise released a breath. It caused the steam from her cup to waver. She took a sip of tea and savored it for a moment. "They said they're busy. They also said you are capable."

"Are you saying they want *me* to do it? Do they know I'm only fifteen?"

My aunt chuckled. "A few days ago, you thought you were practically an adult."

I considered the prospect of fighting a pack of vampires. I considered them tearing out my heart. "Okay, I might have been wrong about that." My voice was quiet, subdued. I didn't like the sound of it.

"They said you're the son of two exceptional agents. They've trained you well and think you're up to the task."

I raised my eyes to meet hers. "Do *you* think I am?"

She held my gaze, then said, without breaking eye contact, "Yes. After what you did to the first one, I believe you are able. But it'll be hard and dangerous. You could die."

"And if we do nothing, others *will* die. Humans."

She considered me for a moment. A slight twitch of her lip broke the tension in her face. "You care about them? About the humans? Even though they would hunt us down if they discovered us?"

"The people here wouldn't. I know their leaders are dangerous. But here in town, they're innocent. And they can't defend themselves. They would be like sheep to the vamps."

"Marta and Dragos have taught you well. Compassion is an important quality."

I shrugged. "It's only right."

Aunt Elise gazed out the window from her seat. Sunlight streamed into the room through the glass. "If the monsters discover there are sorcerers in town, they will come after us."

"Then it's best if we hit them first," I said.

"Of course, we don't even know if there are any more. You might have killed the only one."

"Then it's time to hunt. How can you tell a vampire from a human? They look human, don't they, when they're not hunting?"

Aunt Elise shrugged and sipped again. "I have no idea. We'll both have a lot to learn on this mission."

"You can say that again." Draining the last of the tea, I rose and moved toward the kitchen to put the cup away.

"Malcus," my aunt said as I reached the threshold. "You're not an Alliance agent. You don't have to do this."

"And make you do it all? No way. Besides, it's good training. I'll never know how skilled I am until I put my powers to the test."

In the kitchen, I placed my cup on the counter by the sink, then went upstairs to my bedroom. The thought of fighting a pack of vampires both thrilled and terrified me. But I knew how proud my parents would be if I succeeded in the mission. And I knew how disappointed they'd be if I walked away.

There was no question about it. Whether for glory or death, I would see it through.

Vampires.

I stared out my bay window at the dark and wet street, lit only by streetlights. The yellow orbs of illumination cast an eerie glow about the scene. They provided far too many shadows for my taste. It had rained in the afternoon. Starting around three, it came down in a relentless deluge until a half hour ago. The damp pavement reflected the light in places as I scanned for motion.

Vampires are one of the rare monsters that are both intelligent and evil. Oh, there are plenty of intelligent types out there, and some individuals from each are bad. But the entire *species* of vampire is evil. Every last one. It helps that they're forced to feed on humans to survive. These blood-suckers are usually solitary predators, but they're known to operate sometimes in packs. One or two from the pack would stalk their prey while the rest keep watch to eliminate witnesses. In this way, they can live and hunt without raising suspicion.

Was there a vampire pack in Durbin Point?

It would certainly explain why my parents and Aunt Elise were unaware of them. But the monster's reckless behavior the other night lacked the discipline that comes with pack rules.

How do you discover if there are vampires in your town? They don't fly or turn into bats. They don't sparkle, they aren't inhumanly beautiful. Unless they're hunting, they look like everyone else. Are there any telltale signs?

I didn't know of any. Although I hated the monsters and swore to kill any I found, I honestly never expected to find one. So I kept putting off studying them. After all, I was sure I'd be with my mom or dad when I hunted them.

Mom and Dad.

What would they do? How would they go about finding vampires? They know more about them than I do. They researched them. The library in our house was full of books about vampires and other monsters. My parents would lock themselves in the library and pour over those books until they had the information they needed.

But I didn't have those books. I couldn't teleport back to our house in Colorado. Even if I cast a circle, the distance would be too great. All I could use was what we had in this house.

I looked around my room, hoping to locate a source of information I hadn't thought of yet. My library, an abridged version of what I had at home, took up a single bookshelf that stood against a wall. When I chose the books, I had neglected to include any on mythic creatures, assuming, in error, I would have no need for them.

My laptop computer sat alone on my desk. I frowned. I understood only the rudiments of its use, but research was easy enough. Of course, the Internet was a human construct, and thus all the information available there would consist of popular myths and legend, and not the reality. *Still, it's worth a try,* I thought.

I took a seat at my desk and folded open the computer's screen. With a flash, the display illuminated and presented me with my desktop. I brought up a browser and clicked into the search bar. I considered possible queries and then typed:

How to identify a vampire.

I hit the Enter key and waited. Within seconds, the screen filled with links containing titles like *Dracula to Edward: The Vampire Look, The Vampire Inside,* and of course, *Vampire Boyfriends: Pros and Cons.* It was truly frustrating. But then my eyes landed on a name that caught my interest:

A Sorcerer's Guide to Magic, Monsters, and the Mythic World.

I stared at it, my mouth agape. There it was, in big blue letters on the search page, easily lost among the trivial links to all but a mythic person. As a real sorcerer, that title spoke to me.

Could it be . . .

I clicked the link. The screen went white for a few seconds, and then the title appeared, followed by a page of content that seemed custom tailored to sorcerers. A slide show of news items dominated the top, with titles like *Association Agents Cover up Goblin Raid in Tasmania*, and *Possible Troll Sighting in Bergen, Norway*. Elsewhere were links to sections about the mythic world—the *real* mythic world. The terms were too correct, the hints of information in the links and headlines too accurate.

I was looking at a website made for real sorcerers.

Did the Alliance know about this? I doubted it. If they did, they would have taken it down, and dealt with those who created it. One headline mentioned "Association Agents." *They must be calling the Alliance by that alias.*

My mouse hovered over the menu, and I moved it to the "About" link and clicked. The page changed and was replaced with the following text:

The creators of A Sorcerer's Guide to Magic, Monsters, and the Mythic World *wanted to provide a comprehensive reference and news portal for all sorcerers who live in the human world. Now, you can keep up with current events and learn more about the world you have left behind.*

At the bottom of the page was a note in fine print. I squinted at the screen and read the line:

This site is presented for entertainment purposes. Any similarities to things real or imagined are purely coincidental.

"Hmm," I said to myself. *This is clearly all real, but they inserted this disclaimer so humans would assume it's fake.* "Clever."

I thought briefly of showing this to Aunt Elise, but decided to investigate it further before taking any action. Besides, I needed the site.

I clicked into the site's search box, typed "vampire," then hit the Enter key. A page appeared with a list of monsters in alphabetic order. I scrolled down to the monster I wanted and clicked on it.

The new section began with a description of vampires. These weren't the common descriptions, but appeared to be the real thing. I scanned the text for the information I was looking for, then read.

Identification

Vampires resemble the humans they used to be, and unless they're hunting, they are difficult to identify. Magic Sight is helpful, but not accurate. The monsters have no magical energy of their own. They steal it from their victims. A fully fed vampire will glow as brightly as any human. A hungry one will be dim. Those who are starving will be empty and dark. Most vampires don't let their energy get that low, however. Although Magic Sight can be useful, it's not a guaranteed method of identifying them.

There are some physical tells. A vampire's skin tone is always off. If they have recently fed, their skin will appear redder and darker than most humans. Otherwise, they would be somewhat pale. It's important to note that these differences are subtle, and it's possible to falsely identify a person as a vampire. Fortunately, there is also a behavioral difference that, when combined with the above physical traits, creates an almost complete identification. Vampires always consider humans as prey, so they will be as lions among a herd of antelope. The predators will size up everyone they see, looking for both food opportunities and threats. Weaker and lone humans will gain more attention. Still, extreme care should be taken when identifying a vampire, because one mistake could result in murder.

I sat back and considered this passage, comparing it to what I already knew about the creatures. It fit perfectly and made sense. And it was the best information I was likely to find. I bookmarked the page, then closed my computer screen.

It was time to put my new discovery to the test. Grabbing my coat, I ran downstairs and to the door.

"I'm heading out for a while!" I called as I reached for the doorknob.

"Wait a minute!" Aunt Elise called back.

The breath I let out announced my annoyance as I lowered my hand and waited for her to enter the hallway. She arrived presently and studied my face.

"You're going out to look for them. The pack."

"I have to, like we discussed."

"I know. But it's dangerous. Don't take any unnecessary risks."

"Of course. They won't be in out-of-the-way places. They'll be in public, where they can see more of their prey. That's where I'll be."

"Good. I don't want anything to happen to you, Malcus. Your life is more important than finding those vampires."

"More important than the humans of Durbin Point?" I asked.

"Yes."

I hesitated. Her expression was strong and determined, but the dampness of her eyes betrayed her fear. I put a hand on each of her shoulders and smiled warmly at her.

"I will show extreme caution, Aunt Elise. It's my plan to observe, not to act."

"Okay," was all she managed to say.

I kissed her forehead, then stepped outside into the chill night air. "I'll be back in two hours."

She nodded as I closed the door between us.

On my way down the walkway to the street, I wondered if human parents give their children as much responsibility and freedom as Aunt Elise gave me. Somehow, I doubted it.

Chapter Seven

I walked briskly down Dunmore Street to Church Street, going away from the ocean. This larger road ran straight for a half mile, passing several side-streets that looked identical to mine, until it ended at a rotary in downtown Durbin Point. I would be safe once I reached the lit sidewalk and shops of Main Street, but until then, I felt vulnerable.

Brightly colored leaves lay stuck to the wet concrete and my sneakers smacked loudly with each step. I glanced in all directions as I walked, painfully aware that my own steps would mask those of approaching feet.

I wasn't alone on Church Street. Cars drove by, and I passed several people heading in the other direction. A few smiled cordially, but most kept to themselves with white or black earbud wires dangling like jewelry from their heads. I realized then I had little to fear from vampires that night. With a plethora of humans oblivious to their surroundings as they listened to their music, no vampire would target the only person who seemed acutely aware of his own.

The tension that kept me on guard eased as I approached the buildings that marked my arrival at the town's hub. A brick building rose on my left, with the street to my right. A large picture window dominated the wall as I walked the final dozen steps to the corner. The warm glow of its lights spilled onto the sidewalk to illuminate my path. The coffee shop was busy, and I decided it would be the first stop on my reconnaissance mission. It was chilly out, and the thought of a steaming mug of tea sounded good. I don't drink coffee. I love its aroma, but it's far too bitter. With enough cream and sugar, it was almost bearable, but it would stop being coffee at that point. Besides, tea helps with spell-casting, so it was my favorite drink.

A bell tinkled as I entered and took a moment to scan the room. Three teenagers sat at a large wooden table, text books and laptops open as they typed away with the obligatory headphones covering their ears. Several smaller tables along the walls were occupied by single people reading or playing on their phones while they drank. Two women and a man stood in line, the ladies chatting together while the guy eyed them discreetly as he waited at the end of the queue.

I stepped into place behind him. His interest in the women turned out to be normal, since they were attractive and the man kept looking at their behinds.

Finally, with tea in hand, I left the establishment.

One shop down. No vampires.

Durbin Point had a nice downtown. Their efforts at beautifying its center were a success. Upscale bars and cafes lined the street, and I passed benches and decorative trees that grew beside the road. People walked up and down the sidewalk, visiting the shops and restaurants that remained open at that time. But I failed to see any who matched the *Guide's* description of a vampire. After spending an hour wandering along Main Street, I had serious doubts regarding the veracity of the website. Perhaps it was like all the other sites' made up drivel . . . drivel that, by coincidence, seemed amazingly credible.

A man walked past me as I stood leaning against a tree. Tall and lanky, he moved with a slight swagger, which caught my eye. His face was dirty, light brown hair hanging in greasy strands over his eyes. Stumbling over a poorly inserted cobblestone on the sidewalk, he almost fell but caught himself. He glanced back nervously before continuing his quick, swaying gait.

I noticed three things about the man as he hurried past me towards the darker residential section of Main Street. One, he was clearly homeless, from his shoddy clothes to his ragged appearance. Two, his unsteady gait and unfocused gaze implied that he was drunk. And three, he was afraid.

I remained at my post, but watched him discreetly as he deserted the bright lights of commerce and fell into shadow.

A couple wandered past, also leaving the businesses behind for the subdued atmosphere of apartment houses. The man stood six feet in height, with broad shoulders and short blond hair that made the flush of his skin stand out in sharp contrast. The woman was all curves and grace as she walked along, her arm wrapped lovingly around his. Black hair cascaded down her back and bounced with every step. The fairness of her features looked exotic, with all that blackness cradling her delicate face.

I tensed as they sauntered by, taking casual strides and

laughing together at some shared joke. They appeared to be a handsome young couple in their mid twenties spending a fun evening shopping and enjoying what pleasures Durbin Point had to offer.

The woman beamed up at her beau as she clung to his arm, then glanced with uncharacteristic directness toward the homeless man. Then, in the blink of an eye, she returned to the loving adoration of her companion.

The boyfriend did the same thing, occasionally breaking character to eye the retreating man before returning his gaze to his lover.

I was reminded of a cat who licks its paw in seeming disregard of a nearby mouse, only to snatch quick glances at its prey. This was a game for them. They were playing with their food.

The man's face was flush, red as though with anger. Her skin was pale. And they behaved like predators as they followed the homeless man down the street.

Flush face. Pale skin. Acting like predators. I gasped.

Vampires.

This was exactly how the *Guide* described them. Of course, it might also be unreliable. But I had a hunch. Something inside told me they were monsters.

If they were vampires, then they were hunting as a team, and that poor guy didn't stand a chance.

I had promised Aunt Elise I would only observe and not act. And although I had managed to take out that first vampire, it had left me vulnerable, and there was a moment when I wasn't sure I'd survive. But this was a pair, and they looked smarter and more dangerous.

But I couldn't let them kill that man. I just *couldn't*.

I pulled out my phone and started walking behind the couple. With my Magic Sight, I could see all three of them, the two vampires and the homeless man, a short distance ahead of them. Both monsters had human levels of magical energy, although the man's was stronger.

"Sorry, Dave," I said jovially into the phone as I walked, when the woman glanced back at me. "You'll have to start without me. I just left town. I'll be home in a little while." This satisfied her, and her attention returned to her partner.

It was an odd train of people, the homeless man, the couple, and then myself taking up the rear. We went far down Main Street, passing first apartment houses, and then real homes. Here the streetlights were farther spaced, and a few remained dark, allowing the shadows to encroach upon us.

I had to think of a plan to give the man a chance to escape. I couldn't fight them. Magic was out of the question. I had to do something subtle, something to ruin their opportunity to attack without raising suspicions.

I needed a distraction. Better yet, I needed an *attraction*. A commotion that would bring lots of people around and scare off the monsters. But what? I knew a variety of spells, but I was never one for subtlety. Magic was not the answer.

A group of boys walked loudly on the other side of the street, laughing and shouting and making merry. The couple glanced at them and scowled. I couldn't see them too well in the dim light, but a thought had formed in my mind.

I burst into a jog and, skirting past the vampire lovers, made my way closer to the homeless man, which put me directly across from the boys.

I waved to the gang and shouted. "Hey!"

The kids all stopped. So did the monsters. Their prey, attempting to escape the commotion, quickened his pace and vanished into the shadows. The group of youths turned to face me, and as I opened my mouth to pretend I knew them, I realized with terrifying clarity that I *did*.

Mark and his friends from the arcade stared across the road at me, the bully's face scarlet with anger.

"Rousseau!" I shouted, the words ringing in my head. "It ends here!"

It was all I could think of. I had already played my hand, and what I did had to be believable or the vampires would set their sights on me. In my periphery, I saw the monsters standing there, their gaze floating between the boys across the street and me. All thought of the homeless man had gone. There was nothing to do but continue the spectacle.

The four large brutes crossed the road and stopped before me.

"Are you really that *stupid*?" Mark sneered, and I had my first moment of doubt about my plan.

"Everyone says you're out to get me," I said. "I didn't want trouble, and I certainly didn't *cause* it. But if you're determined to hurt me, for some reason, then let's get it over with. But I'll have you know, I won't go down easy."

The vampires seemed genuinely interested in the turn of events.

Mark regarded me with a strange expression. I saw a mixture of anger, curiosity, surprise, and something else . . .

He nodded with finality. "Okay then."

His fist once again appeared before my eyes, but this time I hopped to one side. I wasn't going to fall for the same attack twice. But I still erred in not mounting an immediate counter-attack. He reacted to my maneuver with far too much skill, and a follow-up strike with his other fist hit me hard in the chest.

I staggered backward with the impact. All the breath had left me, and pain shot from my ribs and spread throughout my body. I tried to steady myself, but my legs became wobbly and I fell onto my backside.

Mark's friends burst into laughter, but their leader silenced them with a growl.

"Get up!" he shouted at me.

I sat there on the cold concrete, my hand on my chest. The pain throbbed, and I wished I had taken the time to learn heal-ing magic. But as much as I wanted to give up the fight, I had the vampires' attention, and I needed to keep it a little while longer. I climbed to my feet, struggling to steady my legs as I took control of my breathing once again.

Mark hung back to let me recover, then moved in. Once again he went for my face, but this time I ducked to the other side, hopped behind him and punched hard in his kidney.

He twisted around and a grimace showed that I had hurt him. But I was trying for more than a grimace. He rushed me, and I fell back, almost tripping over the couple who jumped away at the last second. I was struck, first in the shoulder, then in the stomach, then another on the side of my head. Then I lost count. It wasn't the gang. It was all Mark, and he moved quickly in a dance of fists and ducks and dodges and more fists. I tried my best to block the strikes, but I couldn't. My mind reacted too slowly to the deluge, and I lost more control over my body with each successive hit. After taking far more punches than I should have, I fell to the ground and curled up into a ball.

The punches stopped at that point, and the kicks I expected to feel never came. I hazarded a peek and saw Mark walking to his friends, his back to me. The vampires looked back and forth between the ruffian and me. I couldn't tell how long the fight had been, but I guessed it was pathetically short. And I had no idea if the homeless man had got away. I had to continue the display until I knew.

Slowly and painfully, I rose. My entire body ached, and my legs protested, but I managed to stand up. A quick glance showed no sign of the man, but the two vamps stood nearby, watching me intently.

"Hey!" I said, but it came out more like a croak.

Mark stepped slowly around to face me, his face creased with concern.

"We're done, Molova. It's over."

"So you can save the rest for another day?"

"No. We're good. I won't bother you anymore."

It was now my turn to frown. "Why not?"

Mark shrugged. "You stood up to me. You didn't have to, but you did. I respect that."

He turned and the four of them made to cross the street.

Something hard was placed into my open hand. Looking down, I saw a rock there. The female vampire gently wrapped my fingers around it. My gaze then drifted to her face.

She seemed more beautiful now than she had from a distance. My eyes were trapped in hers like a fly in a web, only I didn't want to escape. I yearned to remain caught in her gaze forever, opening my mind to her and letting her know everything about me. But something wasn't right. As wonderful as it felt to be caressed by her eyes, a nagging thought tugged at my consciousness, telling me to turn away.

"Do it," she whispered.

I looked down at the rock in my hand, then at Mark's retreating back as the gang crossed the street. I will admit, part of me wanted to throw it, to get a final parting shot. To maybe hurt him at least a little.

But I couldn't. Mark had shown me respect after fighting him, even though I lost. I was certain that throwing a stone as he walked away would lose that respect. It went against my ethics.

I opened my hand, and the rock slipped past my fingers to clatter on the concrete.

"I'm done, and I need to get home. People are waiting for me."

She snorted. "Wimp."

The two monsters turned and made their casual way back downtown.

I thought about the experience as I limped painfully toward home. Were they vampires? My only evidence was a vague visual characteristic, and a behavior that might have been anything. The identification instructions the *Guide* gave me were not precise. A lot of people have those skin tones, and I might have seen more in their behavior because I wanted to see it. I could have been completely off base with them.

That is until I felt the woman's hand.

Her fingers were ice cold. There was no way a human would have had fingers that cold and not be in agony. There was no doubt left in my mind.

I had interrupted two vampires on the hunt.

Chapter Eight

"Do you plan to get hurt every time you leave this house?" Aunt Elise smiled as she applied a Band-Aid to my cheek.

"I have no such plans, I promise you." I winced when I dabbed a wet cloth to my nose. It was the second time that week my nose got hit, and both with the same fist. But I felt confident it would be the last. Mark said it was over, and I had no intention of starting it up again.

"And that couple. Are you sure they're vampires?"

"Absolutely."

She stepped back from me to inspect her handiwork. "This is troubling. We're all alone on this, and a pack is beyond our ability."

"I'm up to it."

"I don't think you understand what we're up against."

"Oh, I know perfectly well what we're up against. But I've got surprise on my side."

"I doubt that." She offered me a piece of pound cake. "You

killed one of them, and in the most graphic way possible. You've announced our presence better than if you had handed them a business card."

"They didn't act concerned at all."

"Then they mustn't know, yet."

"If they haven't by now, they never will." I put a forkful of the confection in my mouth, then frowned as I chewed. "Cake at this hour? Isn't it too late?"

"Shut up and eat. It's good for you."

She took the wet cloth from my hand and went to the sink. "Why do you think they won't find out?"

"It was in the woods and we were alone. And vampire bodies dry up and flake away when they die. With all this rain, the remains are long gone. And how is cake good for me?"

My aunt shook her head as she rinsed out the cloth. "I hope you're right. We'll need every edge we can get."

"What do we do now?"

"We find their nest and see how many are in the pack."

I flashed Aunt Elise a look. "That's it? If we find their nest, we can kill them all. A Daylight spell would do the job."

"I'm afraid it won't. Artificial daylight, even from a spell, will have no effect."

"Then we stake them. We can't let them live."

"I'm not suggesting we do," Aunt Elise said. "But we have to use our heads. The nest will be guarded. When their friend goes missing, they're likely to keep a low profile, which means no unnecessary hunting. This gives us the benefit of time. Play it safe, and we can end them. Act rash, and we'll both be dead."

She was right, of course. We had to proceed with caution.

I nodded my agreement as I handed her the empty plate.

"Nice cake," I said.

I felt better by morning. There must have been some recuperative power in Aunt Elise's cooking, as the pain decreased when I ate and my vigor improved. Perhaps there was some real magic to my aunt, after all.

News of the fight traveled fast. Mark's gang spread the word of their friend's victory, and people came to console me or give me their support for standing up to him. I became a hero among the masses, even though I made it clear that Mark had won the fight.

Kathy wouldn't stop talking about it throughout Social Studies, and I came to understand why Oni had done the bulk of the work. It's hard to talk as much as she did and hope to get anything accomplished.

"Why did you challenge him to a fight? Did it hurt real bad? I hear there was a big crowd. That bruise must hurt. Everyone says you're a hero, you know. You're *so* brave!"

It went on like that for the entire class. Tracy said nothing, but she afforded me a wry smile when I looked at her helplessly during the monologue. Even Oni hardly got a word in.

One of Mark's friends, Jake, passed me in a corridor on the way to Spanish class. Many of the students stopped to watch the incident, but looked disappointed when the brute only nodded toward me and continued down the hall.

I had earned the boy's respect. *Mundanes target those they have no respect for, and leave them alone once they gain it. Interesting.* Focusing on the vampires would be much easier if I no longer had to worry about these kids. I wondered if all human gangs worked that way.

Oni was smiling when I joined him in the cafeteria.

"I won't ask any annoying questions about you and Mark. Besides, I got the gist from the few Kathy let you answer."

We both laughed.

I looked around to make sure Brigid wasn't coming, then leaned forward conspiratorially.

"There are more vampires."

Oni's eyes widened, and he hesitated, his burger hovering before his open mouth.

"I went searching downtown and found two of them. They were out hunting. My run-in with Mark was an attempt on my part to distract them from attacking a homeless man."

He recovered from his initial shock quickly. He took a bite as I told my story.

"Did it work?" he asked.

I nodded.

"How did you know they were vampires?"

I explained it, without mentioning the *Guide*.

He considered it for another couple bites of his sandwich, then washed the food down with cola.

"They don't know about their friend yet," he said.

"You think so?" I agreed, but I wanted to hear his explanation.

"They wouldn't have been out hunting in public if they knew something like you was out there."

"I doubt they would fear me."

Oni chuckled. "You didn't stake it through the heart. You blew it apart. Even if you can't do that again, they'll think you can. They'd be afraid."

"Hmm . . . I never considered that. But they shouldn't find

its remains, so they won't know what happened."

"I hope you're right."

"Hey, Brigid's coming," I blurted. She made eye contact and walked my way, her ponytail bobbing behind her. "You tried to tell me something yesterday, but I didn't understand it."

Oni laughed. He laughed longer and harder than I wanted. The girl was halfway to our table and several people were watching us when he finally stopped.

"I was saying she likes you, and you should go for it. Honestly, I thought even *you* would understand that."

I shrugged in response as Brigid took her seat next to Oni.

He got up at once. "Well, I'm off. I'll call you tonight." With that, he walked across the crowded room toward the exit.

"I hope I'm not scaring him away," Brigid said.

"I'm sure you're not." She was, but I felt she might not want the truth in this case.

She stared at my face for an awkward moment and then nodded with satisfaction.

"You don't look too bad. Only a couple of bruises and a few cuts. I expected worse."

"You heard."

"I told you not to get yourself hurt."

"It was unavoidable, I assure you."

"I somehow doubt that." Her words might have sounded like an argument, but her demeanor remained playful. Her eyes twinkled.

I had nothing to say. Her magnificence drew all the words from my mind. I simply stared at her.

"I'm looking forward to Saturday night," she said, changing the subject.

I shook my head vigorously as the thoughts flooded back to me. Had she cast a spell on me? It didn't feel like one. Another bit of mundane girl magic, perhaps?

The date. It was tomorrow night. It was at *night*. Those vampires were hunting downtown, near where I planned to take her.

"We have to change the date. I need it to be during the day, and not at night."

She frowned. This was the first time I had ever seen her frown. She was every bit as beautiful. But all the same, I wanted her to smile back.

"You haven't dated before, have you?" she asked, as though she already knew the answer.

I shrugged. I was confused by that question, so I had no response.

"Nighttime dates are romantic. Daytime dates just, well, *aren't*."

"How is a daytime walk on the beach not romantic?"

She rolled her eyes. "There are more people there. At night, there are fewer people, and they are all couples. And, there is a sunset. Also, I'm sort of a night owl. Please humor me on this one date. Our next one can be in the daytime, I promise."

It was either the passion with which she argued her point, or that she mentioned a "next date" that convinced me.

"All right," I said. "I'll keep it an evening date. I like the night, too. But I have reason to believe it's not safe here after dark." I didn't mean to say it. I blurted it out.

"What do you mean?" She seemed genuinely concerned.

I closed my eyes to collect my thoughts. How could I explain it without saying the V-word?

I regarded Brigid thoughtfully. "I have a knack for spotting danger when others don't. I get it from my parents. They're investigators, in a manner of speaking. I can't explain it to you, and you wouldn't believe me if I tried. You *must* trust me when I say this town is not as safe as it seems. Especially at night."

Brigid watched me as I spoke, and the piercing gaze of those eyes seemed to look right through me.

At last, she sat back and let my eyes go. "You are certainly a man of secrets, Malcus Molova. I'm good at seeing lies, and you told the truth, although you kept a lot out. Is it that important to have our date during the day?"

She accepted it. I knew little about human ways, but I was *certain* she would not have accepted my explanation. In fact, I assumed she would have called off the date and walked away. But she believed me and was willing to acquiesce. Still, she looked disappointed, and I didn't like that.

"Tomorrow night is fine. But we should stick to public places. No back roads, and no secluded spots, I'm afraid."

"What about a dark corner of a busy cafe?" Her playful smile returned.

I grinned. "Now, *that* sounds perfect!"

The buses line up outside the front doors after school, and all the kids line up to board. My bus was usually late and one of the last to pull up. I stood to one side of the great double-door and leaned against the brick wall as I watched the chaos unfold. There were lines of students entering the buses, but social groups formed here and there. They talked excitedly about their day. Others ran around on errands of their own, while still more chose to walk home and strolled away across the parking lot in pairs and groups.

I considered walking home as I watched one group of three kids waiting to cross the street. I could. After all, I knew how to get home, and I had learned all I could about riding the bus.

I was about to begin my trek when I saw him. A man stood across the street and stared at the crowds of students bustling around the school. No. That wasn't right.

The man was staring at me.

Our eyes met, and he looked away. He was nervous, as though he didn't want to be there, and was afraid of getting caught. I continued to watch him as he snuck a few glances my way, then turned to leave.

I was halfway across the parking lot before I realized I was following him. Yet, I didn't change my course. That man had been spying on me, and I needed to know why. He couldn't be a vampire because it was the middle of the afternoon, and the sun shone brightly in the sky. A vampire would have burned to a crisp long before getting to the school.

So, who was he, and why was he interested in me? I aimed to find out.

The man had walked down a side street, and I saw his back retreating when I rounded the corner. A brief look around showed that nobody was in sight, aside from him. I paused for a moment and then went invisible. When there were no cries of alarm, I jogged toward him until I was about ten feet behind and then continued tailing him.

The man's nerves hadn't subsided. He kept looking around as though expecting to get caught doing something nefarious. But all he had done was spy on me. The man wore black slacks, a white shirt, and a tie. His black hair was short but slightly disheveled. A store clerk, possibly? I couldn't tell. I still hadn't done that kind of research. I should go shopping with Aunt Elise sometime.

Why was I following him? I kept asking myself that question. He wasn't a vampire, so why should I care? I looked at him with my Magic Sight. He was alive and glowed with the right amount of energy for a human, though it was a bit low. So, the guy was sick. That wasn't a good enough reason to follow him.

He was spying on me. That was why I stalked after him, invisible and undetected. Sure, the man could have been a human predator after a child. But the likelihood that he would randomly take an interest in the one Mythic kid in the school was too slim to believe. He was interested in me, specifically. And I had to know why.

I drew out my phone and called Aunt Elise. She answered after two rings.

"Hi," I said. "I won't be home right away."

"Why not?" She didn't sound concerned. She probably assumed it was about school.

"A man was spying on me, so I'm tailing him to find out why."

There was a pause on the line, and I was about to repeat what I had said when she spoke. "He's not a vampire, so it could be because you're a sorcerer. Have cast any spells within the past several days that might have been seen?"

"No." I said it right away, but my escape from Mark and company followed that word into my head. "Well, I don't think so."

"Tread carefully, Malcus. There are Mythic people out there who don't take kindly to others of our kind. And you don't know what he is."

"He's not magical. I checked. And he's acting nervous. But I'll be careful."

"Okay. Keep me informed."

"Will do." I hung up and shoved my phone back into my pocket.

The man crossed the street and went into a house. It was a small place with one floor and a tiny yard. An old, small car was parked in the driveway. He used a key, entered through the front door, and then shut it behind him.

I sat down on the curb across the street and started my own spying operation. After fifteen minutes of inactivity, I pulled out my homework and busied myself. I had to be careful not to let any of my stuff lose contact with my body, or it would suddenly become visible.

Detective work turned out to be a lot duller than I had imagined it would be. I sat on the curb for two hours, waiting for something to happen. Then, finally, I pulled out my phone and tried to look up the address to see who it belonged to. None of the sites I could find offered the data without a fee, but one of them said it was home to an F. Richards. But that was the extent of my luck in information gathering.

At last, as evening shadows stretched their way up the street, I packed up my gear and crossed the street to peek in the man's window. Looking inside the front window, I found him in the living room, pacing nervously. He looked anxious. Terrified might be the better word. This mystery was getting stranger by the minute.

A movement made me spin around in surprise. A woman was walking up the path to the front door. She looked in her mid-twenties, with golden blonde hair that cascaded in waves over her shoulders. She was tall and slim with an athletic build. Her expression was stern as she approached me.

And she was a vampire.

I used my Magic Sight as soon as I saw her. She was hungry, according to the low level of energy in her body. That would explain the determined look on her face.

She paid me no mind since I was still invisible and knocked on the door.

Mr. F. Richards jumped then ran to the door. He opened it and flashed a smile that was somehow both joyous and horrified at the same time.

"May I come in?" the vampire asked, her tone mocking. She had no respect for this man. None, whatsoever.

"Yes, Angel," Richards said meekly. He lowered his head and stepped aside.

She entered, and he closed the door.

I'm not a devious person, but I must admit there have been times when I needed to overhear a conversation taking place in another room. I learned a spell that would extend my hearing through any wall I'm touching. I ducked my head below the window and dropped my invisibility. Maintaining two spells like that was possible, but I decided not to overdo it since I needed clarity in the eavesdropping spell. First, I pressed my hand against the wall beside the window. Then, I directed the magic through my body, down my arm, and out into the wall.

"How could you fail me?" The woman's voice was vicious, and I suddenly felt concerned for the man's life. "He's only a child!"

"But he's clever, Mistress. He saw me and got suspicious, so

I had to leave."

"You could have doubled back and followed him."

"By then, I would have missed what bus he boarded. It was very crowded there. Besides, I swear he followed me."

"He did?"

"I saw him cross the parking lot toward me as I left and started down my street. I didn't see him following me, but I'm sure he was there. I could hear him."

There was a pause, and I was sure that the vamp was deciding what to do with the poor man. "Then you did the right thing," she said at last. Her tone was softer now, as though she wanted him to know he did well.

"Will you?" Richards said in a pleading tone. His voice shook as he spoke. "Please?"

"Oh, very well!"

Curiosity overwhelmed me, and I risked a peek through the window. The two sat on the couch. The man had pulled up the sleeve of his shirt and held his arm out to her. She took it and stared at it for a moment like someone would with a fried chicken leg. Then she bent her head and bit into it.

Richards gasped, then his eyes rolled back, and he moaned in ecstasy. The vampire woman bowed her head over the man's limb, her blonde hair spilling over it. I couldn't see her drinking his blood, but I could hear the disgusting sucking noise because my hand still rested on the wall.

"See anything you like?"

I spun around, surprised by the sudden voice beside me. A man stood no more than two feet from me. He was about six feet tall with chiseled features on his handsome face. Broad shoulders supported heavily muscled arms. This man lifted weights. A lot of them. He was staring through the window at the two on the couch, and his expression was one of desire. Did he want the woman or what she was eating? He turned his gaze to me, a smirk pulling at his lips.

The smile faded at once as recognition struck him.

"You!" he hissed and lunged for me.

Vampire though he was, his reaction was too slow. I turned and ran before my identity had fully seeped into his brain. Of course, outrunning a vampire was impossible. Especially one as strong as him. I had no weapons, and my bag bounced clumsily on my back as I ran.

I had to get away from him. And that required magic. Yet, it was vital that he not discover what I was. My mouth worked in a silent incantation as I cast the only spell that came to me.

And the world changed.

Everything slowed to a crawl. Everything except me that is. I had total control over my speed. But I didn't want to leave him in the dust. That would give me away. I tried to maintain the same rate as him but turned and headed in a different direction. Then I released the spell.

The vampire shot past me as I had swerved nimbly away from him. I bolted to the fenced stretch of grass between Richards's yard and the neighbor's. My enemy changed direction and charged once more. But at that moment, I ran behind the fence and out of sight.

The world shifted once more, and I was no longer in that neighborhood. The side door to Aunt Elise's house stood before me, the light glowing in the window promising warmth and comfort. And safety.

I had used the last of my power to teleport home.

The door burst open at once, and Aunt Elise stepped out on the stoop. Her eyes were wet.

"I hadn't heard from you for two hours. You said you'd keep me informed. What happened?"

Aunt Elise still thought of me as a child. And that meant she was waiting for my call. She had been crying, and that was my fault.

"I'm sorry," I said. No other words came to help, so those two were on their own.

The anger and tension that had been building flooded out of her in the release of one long breath.

"Come on. Dinner's ready. You can tell me all about it."

I walked past her through the door, which she closed behind her. Delicious smells wafted from the kitchen, and I went straight to it. We sat at the table and served ourselves in silence. After we had begun eating, I told her what had happened.

"That human, Mr. F. Richards, is a slave to the vampire. She feeds off him without killing and without turning him. There's something in their saliva that's like a powerful drug. He's physically addicted to her and will do anything she says to get his next fix."

I nodded as I took a bite of pot roast. "And there are now four vampires."

"They've taken an interest in you. They assigned Richards to spy on you. I'm afraid your distraction the other night got their attention."

"Do you think they know I'm Mythic?" I asked.

Aunt Elise set her milk down and shook her head. "The male vampire tried to toy with you. He wouldn't have done that if he knew you were Mythic. But you should take care to keep it that way."

"Agreed. So now we know the nest has at least four vampires and one slave. I'll bet they have more junkies working for them."

"I'm sure of it," said Aunt Elise.

Great. Fighting vampires was one thing. Doing it without killing human slaves willing to die for them would make our job a lot harder.

Oni came over after dinner. I showed my friend around the house. He had already seen my bedroom, of course, but we had a guest room and a finished basement. We descended into the basement and Oni wandered around as I turned on the lights.

"Oh! What are these?" Oni had gone to a few boxes that were pushed up against a wall.

I joined him and drew an item from one box. "It's fencing gear. I need to practice."

"You fence?" Oni said, incredulous.

I swung the foil in the air. It made two audible *swishes.* The foil looked similar to a sword, but the blade was thin and flexible.

"Sure." I frowned. "That's not normal for humans, is it?"

He shook his head. "Afraid not. It's an Olympic sport, but most people never even think about it."

That made sense. I learned to fence so I could use my sword for more than rituals. My father said I might need it against monsters, so the more prepared I was, the better.

"Show me what you can do?" he said.

"Okay." We suited up, as it can be a dangerous sport if you don't wear protection. We wore white padded jackets and put on face masks with mesh-like screens. I handed him a foil. There was no sharp edge, and a ball covered the tip to prevent injury.

I took my position, with the side of my body facing him to provide a smaller target, and pointed the sword toward him. He copied me, doing a fair job of it. I then showed him the foot-work of how to advance and retreat, and a few simple thrusts. I then had him move forward and attack. He lunged quickly, awkwardly trying to hit my side with his foil. I neatly parried his blade with mine and performed a riposte, where I lunged off my parry and tagged him with the tip of my foil.

"Cool!" he said. "Now beat *this*!" He charged at me, swing-ing his sword in an arc toward my neck. I knelt, extending my left leg out behind me, so it stretched straight with my right leg bent at a low angle. With a *swish*, his sword passed over my head. I thrust my weapon forward and upward, easily tagging him in his chest, the "blade" bending in a great bow as it did so.

"Whoa!" he said, amazed. "That was awesome!"

"It's called a Passata Sotto; it's one of my favorite moves."

Oni removed his mask. "Is there anything you can't do, Malcus?"

I shrugged. "Talk to humans."

Chapter Nine

I had arranged for Oni to spend the night. The charm I created to make him daze-proof was ready, and I wanted to give it to him. Also, he had many questions about my world and I had several about his. Saturday's date with Brigid weighed heavily on my mind.

Oni and I sat at the dinner table with Aunt Elise. She had prepared a terrific meal of chicken cordon bleu, and we focused on eating. The food was delicious and kept my friend quiet for some time. But eventually, his curiosity overcame him. He stole careful glances at first me and then my aunt between bites.

"Okay, I've got to bring it up," he said at last. "This whole supernatural thing. I want you to tell me more about it."

Aunt Elise smiled and nodded. "Of course. Now that you're part of our world, it's only fair we fill you in. What would you like to know?"

"Well," he said tentatively, unsure if he was overstepping his bounds. "You said you're both sorcerers, and you're not human.

Then there are vampires. Are there other types of supernatural beings? And how many are evil?"

Aunt Elise pondered his questions. "There are other types of mythical people. More than you'd think. They try to hide themselves from humans for self-preservation. Not many of them are evil. Just as there are good and bad humans, there are good and bad members of most mythic peoples."

Oni took a sip of milk. "What kinds are there?"

"Most of the species you hear about in mythology. Goblins and fairies, satyrs and centaurs, and so on."

"And they're all walking around among us, like you two are?"

I chuckled. "No. Most of them can't blend in as well as we can. Though some use magical charms to disguise themselves. But even sorcerers tend to keep themselves separate from humans, choosing to live on the outskirts of civilization. My family lives closer to humans than most, but even we live out in the wild and rarely interact with people. That way, there's less chance for someone to see us do magic. Aunt Elise lives here because she can get away with it. She doesn't have magical abilities."

An eyebrow raised on my aunt's face as she turned toward me, her head tilting slightly. "Is that what you think, Malcus?"

I shrugged. "I've never seen you use magic."

"That doesn't mean I can't."

Her response made no sense to me. How could a person have magical abilities and not use them? But I chose not to press the point with a guest there.

She turned her attention back to my friend. "You see, Oni, the consequences of our people being discovered is so great that most sorcerers shy away from humans, even though they could live among them. I believe there's danger in us forsaking your culture, so here I am acting as a quiet observer of the human condition."

"You avoid using magic to keep from being caught," Oni said. That was intuitive of him. It didn't work that way, though. A sorcerer can't suppress the magic. It would come out one way or another. Aunt Elise would have to use her power, if she had any.

"Something like that," Aunt Elise said. Clearly, she didn't want to get into details with my friend.

"How is Malcus adjusting to school?" she asked, changing the subject.

Oni laughed. "He needs to learn more about humans. But he's doing okay. I've helped him make some friends."

"Have you met this girl he's dating?"

"Hey!" I said. I did not approve of them discussing my love life.

Oni laughed again. "Don't worry, Malcus. Everyone in school knows. Your aunt might as well know, too. Her name's Brigid. She's hot—pretty, that is. She joins us at lunch."

"And you run away every time she shows up," I interjected.

"I'm trying to help you out, man!"

Aunt Elise chuckled. "And do you think her intentions are honorable?"

Oni's eyes widened at the turn the interrogation took. "Um, well, I guess so. I mean, they haven't even kissed." He shot me a imploring look. "Right?"

I frowned. My face burned, and I wished I could change the subject. "Of course not! We're just friends."

"But you have a date," Oni said. "Tomorrow night."

"Wait a minute," Aunt Elise cut in. "Tomorrow *night?* I thought you changed it to a daytime date."

"Well, she didn't like that," I said, now feeling squeamish. This was not a comfortable discussion, and it ruined my appetite. "So, we agreed to stick to public places."

She shook her head slowly, her face creased into a frown. She wasn't old, as aunts go, but her expression made her appear so. "You know the danger. You're not safe in public. Nobody is."

"They can't daze me, so I'm fine."

"You're not fine. And they *can* daze her."

"I'll be with her the whole time."

"Will you? Can you really say that?" Her eyes bored into me, and I had the distinct impression she was setting me up for some revelation.

"Of course I can."

"One of the vampires is a woman."

"So?"

"Can *you* use the ladies room?"

Understanding flooded my mind, and I hesitated; a tactical blunder that nearly cost me the argument.

She sat back, satisfaction spreading across her face. Now she looked her age. The thirty-one-year-old sorcerer considered me with that I-got-you look, then gave her ultimatum.

"Call her. Change the time."

I shook my head vigorously. "I was lucky enough to get the date in the first place. I tried to change it once and failed. If I try again, I might drive her away."

Her victory faded from her face, but she didn't appear angry. She drew out a long breath, and it made her bangs move.

Oni smiled at her.

"Okay. But you stick to public places. Stay downtown."

"I will."

"And I'll be there."

"What?" I exclaimed. "You can't!"

Aunt Elise shook her head. "I don't mean I'll join you on the date. I'll follow you at a discreet distance. If she goes to the restroom, I will, too."

"You can't fight a vampire."

"I don't need to. They won't be brash enough to attack two people in the public restroom of a busy restaurant. I have to be there."

I grimaced. There was no way I could win this argument. Her logic was too strong.

"Fine," I said at last, admitting defeat.

"Hey," Oni said to my aunt, a big grin on his face. "Could I come with you?"

"I can't believe she's going to spy on my date," I said once I closed the door to my room. Oni turned toward me after scanning the layout of the place, the insufferable grin still on his face.

"I can't believe you have a date with Brigid Talog."

"Why not?"

"Haven't you seen her? Because *everyone* wants to go out with her. And you're only a freshman."

"She is, too. And I doubt everyone wants to date her."

"Again, have you *seen* her?" Oni said. He seemed surprised that I didn't take his meaning. She was pretty, all right, but not so pretty that every boy in school would want her. "Even seniors ask her out."

I frowned. "Really?" I pictured her in my mind. She had a beautiful face, and her figure was amazing, but there were plenty of gorgeous girls in the school. I meant no offense to Brigid, but Oni was making her out to be impossibly beautiful.

Then I remembered those boys who fawned over her during Gym class. They did it every day. And people stared at her as she walked to join us in the cafeteria.

A sudden idea struck me.

"Oni," I said, my eyes narrowing suspiciously. "How long has Brigid been at the school?"

His eyes darted around the room as he thought it over. "Since the semester started; that was last month."

"Right. How long has she been in Durbin Point?"

"I don't remember her until this year. Why? What are you saying?"

"That Brigid might be a mythic person."

Oni gasped. "You mean she could be a *vampire*?"

"No. She's in school during the day."

"Oh, right. Although, I'd almost say she sparkles."

I leveled Oni with a don't-be-stupid look, but the chuckle struggling to come out betrayed me. With my special hatred of vampires, I've read most books humans wrote about them. Some came surprisingly close to reality. Others . . .

"Okay, okay!" Oni held up his hands in surrender. "Why do you think she's mythic?"

"Well, you see her as being inhumanly beautiful, as though everyone is out of her league. And I've seen other boys act like idiots around her, doing whatever they can to impress her."

Oni considered that for a moment. "Hmm, you're right. I

can't picture any guy being good enough for her. And guys do go nuts over her. She's in my English class. They're always disrupting the lecture to flirt with her. She gets embarrassed."

"She does?" I asked. That surprised me. All the mythic people I knew of that could seduce men like that enjoyed it.

"Yeah. She always buries her head in her book, or gives the teacher a sorry look."

"That cinches it. Brigid Talog is mythic."

"Is she good or bad, though? I hope she's good."

"So do I, because I have a date with her."

"Now, you don't seem to be going crazy over her, like the rest of us. Why is that? Is it some sorcerer ability?"

I shrugged. "Kind of. I'm often not affected by mind spells. A strong one might get me, but most have no effect."

"I bet that's why she likes you!" Oni said. "She's probably sick of the ones who fall for the spell."

"That could be. Or she likes my personality."

"Oh, yeah, that's gotta be it!" Oni said, then laughed. I joined him.

He unrolled his sleeping bag on my floor, then sat cross-legged on it. "What are you going to do about it?"

"There's not much I can do right now. I'll have to keep my eye on her and see. If I can gather more information about her, then I might figure out what kind of creature she is."

"Your mission is to go out on dates with Brigid, as many as you can, to find out what she is. Kissing her would give you some important information, don't you think?"

I laughed. "Definitely! I'd say it's a *must*."

We changed into our pajamas and sat in my room eating snacks and talking about school. We shared a bag of cheese puffs and assorted candy bars, both supplied by Oni. Aunt Elise brought us some home-baked cookies, which we devoured. Eventually, conversation made its inevitable way to vampires.

Oni sat at the bay window, staring out at the darkened street. It was once again raining, this time only as a light mist visible in the glow of the streetlights. A low fog had settled on the ground, adding a somber tone. I had just returned from a fruitful search for more snacks and noticed that my friend no longer smiled as he leaned his head against the glass.

"What's wrong?" I placed the plate on the sill.

Oni sighed and took a cookie. He nibbled at it, his gaze never straying from the scene on the street.

"I'm scared. I used to love going for walks at night. My parents feel safe here and think it's okay for me to wander some. They said I have to learn how to live with more freedom. I would ride my bike everywhere. I'd walk on the trails in the woods after dark and listen to the animal noises. But those days are over."

I knew where this was going, and I had nothing to say that could cheer him up.

"Now I'm afraid to leave my house. I even have my mom walk me to the bus stop in the morning. Do you know what that's like? It's humiliating."

"You're ashamed of your mother?"

"No!" His brow wrinkled when he said it. "Kids think you're a baby if you need your mother to walk you to school. It shows that I'm scared."

"Ah, I see."

"How can you tell a vampire when you see one?" Now he had come to the point. And it was time for his gift.

I told him the things to look for that I had learned from the *Guide* as I went to my desk. I opened the top drawer and removed a crystal pendant on a rawhide string, then returned to the window.

"But that's not enough," I said. "It helped me identify the two I saw downtown, but I wasn't sure until I touched one. She was pale, so she hadn't fed in a while. Her hand was like ice."

Oni sighed. "I was hoping for more than that. I guess I thought if I could recognize them, I might feel safe going outside again."

"You should wait until we've killed the pack before doing that again. At least at night. It would be safe then. But in the meantime . . ."

I held the pendant out to Oni by the string, letting the crystal dangle.

His brow furrowed again. "What's this?"

"A charm. I burned a spell into it. When you wear this, no vampire can daze you. It can try, but you will always have your wits with you when in their presence. It won't identify them for you, but you won't be an easy victim."

He sat up and took the string from me, staring at the crystal in awe. "You're serious? You put a *real* spell on this? I'll be safe from vamps when I wear it?"

"No . . ." I said. "They're still dangerous even without their dazing ability. They have inhuman strength and agility. And, they're hard to kill."

"Yeah, you told me all that. But I'll feel a lot better with this thing handy." He put it around his neck and let the crystal fall to his chest.

Oni grabbed the plate of cookies and left the window. Sitting cross-legged on his sleeping bag, he stuffed another treat into his mouth.

"How do you plan to find them all?" he asked.

I shrugged, climbing onto my bed. "I suppose I'll loiter downtown and watch for the two I know, then follow them. They should lead me back to their nest."

"And what if they attack someone before they go home?"

It took a long time to answer him. The truth was, I had considered that possibility, and I still wasn't sure. That is, I knew what I *had* to do, but I wasn't confident I could do it.

"I'll have to let them kill." It came out in a near-whisper, as I was reluctant to say it. In a stronger tone, to convince myself more than Oni, I continued. "If I intervene, it'll ruin everything. I won't be able to follow them home, and I'll lose the element of surprise. More people would die as a result."

Oni looked at me with concern etched on his face. "But can you do that?"

"I don't know."

I lay in bed, unable to sleep. All was quiet, only the rhythmic pattern of Oni's breathing penetrating the night's stillness. I wasn't prone to insomnia. No, my thoughts kept me awake. Vampires, Brigid, and the enigma of *A Sorcerer's Guide to Magic, Monsters, and the Mythic World* vied for my attention. I gazed across the room at my computer. The *Guide* was there, out on the Internet, where anyone, human and mythic alike, could see it. The website had real descriptions of supernatural creatures, and that was dangerous enough. Did it cover mythic *people* as well? Was there anything about sorcerers? The *Guide* was apparently made for us, according to its title. But did it give the mundane world factual information about us?

I climbed carefully out of bed and tip-toed my way to the computer. There, I sat at my desk and opened the laptop's screen. I then brought up the *Guide*. The site appeared in all its glory. Before, I had gone straight for the search field. This time, I scanned the main page. A slide show dominated the top, each slide containing news topics with pictures and text. The first depicted a gigantic bird, similar to an eagle, but of massive size. The headline read: *Roc sighted over the Montana badlands.* Curious, I clicked on it.

An article appeared with the same title. With mounting trepidation, I read the piece silently to myself.

A roc was seen by twenty-five mundanes yesterday afternoon at 4:20 p.m. A group of paleontologists were working on a dig in the badlands when a great shadow passed soundlessly overhead. They looked up to see a bird the size of a small airplane flying above them. "The bird resembled an eagle, but it wasn't. Its markings were different. And it was gigantic, easily as big as a Cessna." Six people photographed the creature, and at least two of them were uploaded to the Internet. Fortunately, none of the pictures showed anything that could be used to identify scale, so their claims of its size cannot be proven. Association agents diffused the situation using misinformation and skeptical posts online, so that people would not take the sightings seriously. Their work was effective, as it caused a host of skeptical posts and comments from mundanes. The credibility of the sightings was damaged enough to prevent any legitimate investigation.

I stared at the article in surprise. It resembled a normal

newspaper article, but written specifically for sorcerers. And it was in the public domain, visible to *everyone*, including mundanes. And they even mentioned the Alliance, albeit by alias. I searched the website for the owner and history, but found nothing.

"Wait, a minute!" I whispered. "Sorcerers. I need to find out what they say about us." I clicked in the search field, typed "sorcerer" and hit Enter. I was treated to a large list of references to sorcerers, but no page that defined them. I then searched for "gnomes," and "fairies," and even "satyrs," but again found only references. The website described *creatures* and other magical things in great detail, but avoided describing and defining mythic *people*.

The *Guide* also left out anything regarding "the Association," as they called it. They mentioned it now and then, but made no attempt to define or explain it, as though expecting all readers knew what it was.

I sat back, relieved. The website was safe enough regarding sorcerers. A great weight lifted from my shoulders and I relaxed a little. If they had any details about us, I would have had to show the site to Aunt Elise. As it was, I decided to keep it a secret for a little while longer. I had use for it, and I didn't want her to have it shut down or anything like that.

I stared at the screen, wondering what else I could search for. My mind strayed back to the encounter with the vampire couple. I couldn't get over the feeling I had when the woman put that rock in my hand. Clicking in the search field, I typed "vampires hypnotize," then hit the Enter key. The screen changed and displayed a few links to articles from the site. I clicked on one that looked promising and scanned the article.

It was a Q&A page on vampires. About halfway through, I found the following entry:

Q: It's common knowledge that vampires can't hypnotize their prey, only daze them. But a vampire hypnotized my father and made him do terrible things! It was like he fell in love with her. Can a vampire hypnotize their victims?

I gasped. This was exactly how I felt when the woman had put the rock in my hand. When our eyes met, it was as though she were the most amazing thing in the world, and I wanted to do anything for her. *Anything.* It was all I could do to resist her, and when I did, my desire for her suddenly broke and there was nothing. With mounting excitement, I read the answer:

A: It wasn't her vampiric abilities that let her hypnotize your father. She must have been a mythical person before she was turned into a vampire. Sorcerers who become vampires will lose most of their powers, but not all of them. A few abilities would remain. It's rare for a mythic person to become a vampire. Most can't, but some, like sorcerers, can be turned. They always become the most danger-ous vamps possible.

That had to be it. That woman vampire had tried to hypno-tize me, and I almost failed to break it. That was strong magic, something a vampire wasn't supposed to have. She was a mythic person before being turned. She *had* to be!

I closed the screen and returned to bed. That should make her more powerful than the other vampires in her pack. It probably meant she was their leader. And it also meant I wasn't completely immune to her powers. I had gone to the computer to help me relax, but instead it ensured I wouldn't get much sleep that night.

Chapter Ten

Oni spent much of the day with me. After sleeping over, it seemed natural he would hang around. We slept late, had breakfast, and then did our homework together to get it out of the way. I found the work easier to finish when I had someone to discuss it with. I was unused to this team-based work ethic that humans seemed to value.

"We should look at a map," Oni said as we focused on an algebra worksheet.

I flashed him a quizzical look. "For math?"

"No!" he chuckled. "To find the vampires. A map of the town might give us some ideas."

"Hmm." That sounded like a good idea. "I don't think we have any town maps here."

Oni laughed. "You have a computer. For someone with all your mysterious knowledge, you are completely clueless about obvious things. We can find maps of Durbin Point online and even get a street view."

"Street view?"

"You know, where you can see real pictures of the sides of streets. They've mapped out all cities and most towns that way. We could 'walk' our way around town without even leaving the house."

"That sounds useful! You'll have to show it to me."

We went to my room once our homework was done. Oni sat at my desk and navigated easily to the website. He pulled up a map of Durbin Point, NH, then bookmarked it.

"Okay," he said, craning his head to face me as I looked over his shoulder. "Where should we look?"

I frowned. "I'm not sure. I don't know where a pack of vampires might live. And I'm new in town."

"Well, they'll need room and privacy." He smiled and clicked on one spot on the map. "I know of a place." Zooming in over and over, the map stretched, becoming quite large. The line of the street widened into a road, with the name "Harrison Street" written on it. Then, with a final click, the map vanished, and an image of a street appeared before us. It was a residential neighborhood, and must have been Harrison Street. It was a daylight shot, taken in what appeared to be spring, since it was wet from rain yet devoid of fallen leaves. The houses that I could see looked old. White arrows were superimposed over the picture to tell the user where to click.

"You think they own a house?" I asked, skeptically.

"Hold on." Oni clicked on the right-pointing arrow and the image changed to a full view of the house to the right of the original image. Another click, and we were looking down the length of the street in the opposite direction. Oni clicked the forward-aimed arrow a few times, then turned the perspective to frame a particular house.

It was large, an old gambrel, with two gables on the top floor and a porch that ran the length of the house below them. But I could see what Oni meant right away. The place was in bad shape. Gray paint peeled on all the walls. The grass of the small front yard was long and brown, the concrete walkway was cracked, and the front steps looked rickety. But the windows were the giveaway: they were boarded up.

It was an abandoned house.

"It's still like this?" I asked.

"Oh, yeah."

"What made you think of it?"

"I walk by it all the time. I don't live on this road, but it's not far from my home. I get the creeps when I pass it. Like it's haunted, or something."

"I'm not sure an entire pack could live in an abandoned house and not be noticed," I said.

"It's worth checking out, anyway. I mean, it's a start. The vampire that attacked me was all dirty, like a homeless man. And homeless people tend to shack up in houses like this."

I nodded. "We should investigate. As soon as we can."

"How about now? It's not far. We could walk there in about ten minutes."

"Really?" A daylight reconnaissance would make sense. I glanced at the clock by my bed. It read 11:35 a.m.

"You shouldn't come," I said. "It might be dangerous."

"Dude, there is no way I'm staying away. You'd have to tie me up to keep me here. If there are more vampires, I want to know, and I want to *help*."

"But you can't help. I'm sorry, but even with your charm, a

vampire would be too strong for you."

"I'm tougher than you think. And I'll hide behind you, if I have to. But I'm coming. Having another set of eyes and ears, and someone to call your aunt for help, is important. And if we have to escape, I know my way around that neighborhood."

I considered his argument. He had a point.

I let out a breath of resignation. "Okay, but I'm in charge."

"You're the boss!" Oni said with a salute and a grin.

The walk was easy, and I enjoyed the fresh air, even though it blew in cold from the coast. The overcast sky refused to dump its rain on us, and we had a good conversation as we made our way down side streets until we found ourselves at the junction of Harrison Street.

The road looked as it had on the computer, save for more color. Trees grew in most of the yards, and the mid-fall foliage brightened the place with its yellows, reds, and oranges.

We walked down the street to the house in question. The windows were still boarded up; the grass was still long and dead, and the building looked as decrepit. There was no For Sale sign, so it appeared simply abandoned.

The two of us stood on the sidewalk before the cracked walkway that led to the front porch and stared at the house.

"What now?" Oni asked.

"We enter the place."

He frowned. "Um, how do you plan to do that?"

I smiled. "Would you like to see some magic?"

He flashed me an excited look. "Duh!"

"I'll take that as a 'yes.'" I walked across the yard to the side of the house. Short windows near ground level gave a view into the house's basement or they would have if they weren't so dirty. As it was, we only saw darkness through the blur of dirt and dried mud. Looking up, I discovered that the two first-floor windows were boarded up. The two on the second floor were available, with only glass preventing entrance.

"Which do you want? Basement or second floor?" I waited for his response.

He looked first at the small basement window, then up at the others before turning his gaze to me.

"The second floor's a little less scary."

I nodded. "Now, let me concentrate." I shouldn't have given him a choice. Getting to the second floor would require more effort and energy. But I agreed the basement was not the best choice of entrance to a possible vampire lair.

I focused on the second-floor window and my desire to reach it. As I thought about it, my sight blurred for a moment and I knew the spell was working. I envisioned the window sliding down to meet us at ground level. The structure of the house stretched and contorted soundlessly to accommodate the moving window, which glided along like a boat on a sea of wall, finally stopping at its destination before me.

I reached out to the window glass. The clear pane appeared to melt before my eyes, then evaporate away.

Smiling, I stepped through the opening of the window into an old bedroom. I glanced back and saw Oni staring with un-mitigated awe at the open portal.

"Come on," I urged. "I can't keep this up forever."

That snapped him out of his reverie, and he stepped quickly through the window and joined me in the bedroom.

I released the spell; with a disconcerting flurry of silent activity, the window glass returned to its normal state and the scenery outside moved to show us in our proper place, one story above the ground.

I smiled at Oni, who stared at the window with eyes wide and jaw agape.

"How was that?"

"That. Was. *Amazing!*" He shook his head as though to clear his mind and turned to face me. "Did all that happen? Did the window really slide down like that?"

"Perception is a powerful phenomenon. A person who believes he's having a heart attack can suffer the symptoms as though they were real. A talented sorcerer can allow a person to walk through a second-floor window if he believes it's a hole in front of him."

Oni frowned. "So, the house stayed the same, and it was us that moved?"

I shrugged. "Something like that."

I scanned the room. It was clearly a bedroom, but there was no bed, and the only piece of furniture was a bureau so old it looked as though it would fall apart if I pulled on a drawer knob. Dingy paisley wallpaper peeled in places, and cobwebs hung from all the corners. The floorboards creaked even as I shifted the weight on my feet.

I exchanged glances with Oni, who shrugged.

"Doesn't look promising," I said.

"Yeah. Kind of a let-down after that entrance."

We walked to the door, which was already open, the light from our window spilling into a dimly lit hallway.

I paused on the threshold. "I should probably remind you that vampires can be awake during the day, as long as they stay in the dark."

Oni glanced at the darkened hallway, then back at me. "You *could* have said that outside. And we don't have any weapons."

With a pang frustration, I pictured the rapier on its display in my bedroom. I closed my eyes for a moment as I came to grips with my mistake. Then I grinned. "We have *me*."

"That's not encouraging."

"Remember our entrance? I'm not weak, Oni."

My friend nodded. "Good point. Let's get this over with."

I stepped carefully into the hallway. Running the length of the house, it had only two windows, one at each end. They were both boarded up. The floor was carpeted, and the walls had more of the peeling wallpaper. No furniture lined the edges, and no pictures were hung there. The macabre silence intensified in the claustrophobic space, lit only by small patches of light coming in through doorways.

Death.

I smelled it right away, even before my eyes adjusted to the low light. Something dead was in this house; its putrefaction filled the building with a stench I was unfortunately familiar with. I had once helped my parents dispose of a dead ogre in Washington State. Oni grimaced and covered his nose when he joined me in the hallway, but said nothing.

We walked down the hall, one slow step at a time, looking first into one bedroom, then another. They were all the same; empty, save for broken or discarded furniture, dust, and cobwebs. The upstairs windows were not boarded up, so each room was lit too much for a vampire to stand. If vampires lived here, as the odor would indicate, they'd be downstairs or in the basement.

I paused at the top of the stairs. It was pitch dark, with a wall on both sides. The door at the bottom was closed. A vampire could be through that door. I had nothing to stake sleeping vamps with, and no spells ready. I could summon my sword, but it had a long way to fly to get to me, and I'd need an open window to catch it through. I could teleport back home to get it, but that would use all my power. As useful as that spell is, it takes far too much energy to cast. And my showy reality-bending entrance had used a lot of my power already. I realized now that might have been a mistake. A simple levitate spell would have sufficed.

But this was a reconnaissance mission. We weren't planning to stake any vampires we saw, only to verify they were there. And if we encountered any, I could push them out of the way and get us out of the house, pronto. If we were caught, I'd grab Oni's arm and teleport out.

Right.

I set my foot tentatively onto the top step. *Creak!* So much for the element of surprise. Noisy as they were, the stairs seemed sturdy enough, so the two of us descended to the first floor.

The stench of decay grew stronger as we approached the bottom landing. Whatever it was had been dead for a week or so. I paused at the door and listened. There was nothing. All was quiet.

I turned the knob and slowly pushed the door open. Like everything else in this house, it creaked, dragging a grimace onto my face.

It was a kitchen. The appliances were long gone, and some cupboards lacked doors. A small table sat in a corner with four chairs around it. I crossed to the only other door in the farthest corner. I had expected the body I smelled to be there in the kitchen. Now I had to prepare myself for the gruesome sight in each room until I found it. I took a deep breath, which made me cough from the stench, and stepped through into what had been a living room.

Something charged from the shadows and plowed into me, sending me flying back into the kitchen to crash among the table and chairs. Pain surged through my back, arms, and head, but I shrugged it aside as I struggled to extricate myself from two wooden chairs. The vampire, which the attacker must have been, had separated me from Oni, so I couldn't teleport us away. And my friend was now at its mercy.

Kicking one chair across the room and pushing myself to my feet with the other, I turned to face my adversary. It was male, about five and a half feet tall, or it would have been if it didn't stand with a hunch. Its face was white, and it had the upturned nose, pointed ears, and huge pupils that signified its bat-like hunting transformation. But what struck me was its condition. Its greasy black hair hung limply over its head, obscuring parts of its face. Its skin was filthy, matching the rags that had once been clothes, now hanging in tatters from its body. This monster had not tried to blend in with humanity for a long time.

Oni was on the other side of the room, near the door we entered through. He stood on guard, looking loose and at ease. The only thing betraying his calm were his eyes. The vampire stood in the doorway to the living room and snarled at my friend, and I frantically struggled to prepare a spell, any spell that could distract the monster. But I drew a blank. The grand entrance I had made had depleted enough of my power to prevent me from blasting the vamp with pure energy, and nothing else came to mind. I rarely saw action like this; my parents were always there to do the heavy lifting. This gave me a severe disadvantage in the fight.

The vampire charged, and I knew Oni was doomed.

Except he wasn't.

His arms swung in a graceful arc as he stepped to one side, and the monster shot past him, became airborne, and crashed back-first into the cupboards above the sink behind Oni. The boy ran across the room to the living room doorway, neatly changing places with the vamp.

The monster climbed off the counter-top and snarled, its ugly, bat-nosed face twisted in rage.

I made to join Oni, but he shook his head and waved me away. I stopped, out of reflex, as the vampire ran at him once more.

Again the monster ran at Oni, and again my friend's arms drew an arcing pattern in the air. The vampire flipped and struck the wall with its back, its legs off the ground.

But this time, a knife protruded from the creature's chest.

The monster slumped to the ground, dead.

I stared, my jaw agape, at my friend. "How?" was all I could say.

He merely shrugged. "Aikido. My dad teaches it."

"But where'd the knife come from?"

"I saw it in the sink; thought I might need it."

He looked down at the body on the floor. "It *is* a monster, right? I mean, I didn't just murder someone?"

I put my hand on his shoulder. "You did the right thing. It

was definitely a monster and needed to be killed. I would have."

I removed the knife from the vampire. Blood welled up at the wound, but that was it. Just enough to wet its chest. It had been a long time since it had fed. The monster's body changed as soon as the blade was free from its chest. It dried up quickly, turning the corpse into a husk, like a mummy with no wrappings.

"See!" I said. "A monster."

I handed the weapon to Oni. "You might still need this."

The rest of the house was empty. Two coffins had been set up in the basement, both unoccupied. By the signs, the now-deceased vamp had been living here with one other, and I had a strong suspicion it was our friend from the forest. One of the coffins hadn't been slept in for several days. Also, that vampire had been in a similar condition to this one.

After searching the basement in vain for anything that could give us the whereabouts of the pack, I took Oni's hand, and we teleported back to my bedroom.

"We're not any closer to finding the pack," Oni said as he flopped down heavily on my bed. "Are you sure there is one?"

I took a seat on the bay window and gazed out at the street below. "No. I'm not sure about anything anymore. The vamps at that house. There were only two of them. And I saw two others downtown. But there's no evidence that both pairs of monsters were connected. I wish I could have interrogated it."

"I *did* do wrong." Oni frowned, his eyes wet. Killing the vampire had gotten to him, and I realized that he had probably never killed anything before. The truth was, neither had I, until the other night in the woods. But to me, a vampire wasn't like a person. It wasn't even like an animal. It was a monster, something terrible that deserved death. To Oni, it must have felt like he killed a person.

"Listen . . . you did the right thing. It was going to kill us. What you did was self-defense. You had no choice."

"But you wanted to talk to it."

"There was no way that was going to happen. In reality, we couldn't capture it. I wasn't strong enough. I should never have done that flamboyant spell. It was cool and showy and drained me of most of my power. It takes fuel to do magic, and I was running on empty. Staking it was the only thing we could do."

"I've never killed anything before." He looked at his lap, unable to meet my eyes.

The breath that came out of me was not of frustration, but from understanding. I had to say something. He needed to understand that he didn't commit murder, that his act was just.

"One of my spells is called Magic Sight. It gives me the ability to see everything through the perspective of their magical energy. Everything that has magical energy inside it glows, even if it can't do magic itself. All living things have magical energy. People have it stronger than most animals."

Oni sat there, unmoving, still unable to look at me. "You're talking about Ki."

"Exactly!" I said. "Do you believe in the soul, Oni?"

He shrugged. "Yeah, of course. I guess."

"Animals have more magical energy in them than plants because they have a soul. And humans have more of this energy than most."

I paused to let that sink in.

"Do you know how I knew the person who jumped you in the forest was a vampire?"

Oni shrugged, but said nothing.

"He had no energy."

My friend looked up at me. He still frowned, but there was a spark in his eyes. Hope?

"He was a dim shape moving in a place full of energy. And he went to the one thing that had the most. You. You see, although sorcerers believe vampires are alive, it's a known fact they have no soul. Their hearts beat, and they breathe air, but they're not alive in the truest sense. They steal the energy from those they kill. They steal your soul and use it up like food. Then, they will glow for a time with their stolen power, until they've used it up again."

"Really?" Oni wiped tears from his eyes as he looked at me. "So they *are* undead?"

"Sort of. Their bodies are alive, and they can think and talk. But with no soul of their own, they aren't *truly* alive. Not like you and me. So, yeah. Killing a flower is more of a moral dilemma than dispatching a vampire, even though the flower can't talk."

One corner of Oni's lips tugged at a smile. "Are all monsters like that? No soul?"

I laughed. "Watch it! Technically, I'm not a monster. As far as I know, vampires are the only mythical creatures without magical energy of their own."

"It's as though I didn't kill anything."

"Exactly. In fact, you *saved* lives."

"Yeah," he said carefully. He wiped his nose with his sleeve, then grinned. "I'm a hero!"

Chapter Eleven

I had a date to prepare for, so Oni left shortly after our adventure. He said he would do some more research to find a possible hideout for the pack, if one even existed. I wondered about that. Could it be that the town was populated by two pairs of vampires with no real connection to each other? I doubted that. They must know about one another and have some relationship. Perhaps these two had been kicked out of the pack? That was possible.

But I had to push that from my mind. Tonight was my date with Brigid, and my nerves set in. I didn't have anything good to wear, so Aunt Elise took me out shopping in the late afternoon. Although she wasn't old, being only thirty-one, I still assumed she was out of touch with teen fashion. However, since I was woefully lost in that arena, I deferred to her. In the end, I wore clothes that appeared much like my own style, only newer and better fitting. I wore black slacks and a black dress shirt, left open to reveal a white shirt underneath. I wanted red, but Aunt

Elise thought that would be too flashy. We finished with a pair of black sneakers. "You *are* still a boy, after all," she said.

"Now, about your jacket," she said as she examined me. I liked my jacket, but it was rather plain and weatherworn.

"How about a nice cloak?" I offered.

She gave me a wry look. "People don't wear cloaks."

"They don't? That's a shame. I rather like them."

Aunt Elise bought me a wool coat in a style reminiscent of a Navy peacoat. "It's a little out of the ordinary," she said. "But it's you."

At last, I was ready. The plan was to meet her in front of Fratelloni's, a nice Italian restaurant downtown. I had offered to pick her up, with Aunt Elise driving, but Brigid declined. "I can meet you there."

"Do you still plan to follow us tonight?" I asked as Aunt Elise navigated the side streets towards downtown. The neighborhoods went from nice large houses to duplexes, and finally to apartment houses as we made our way to Main Street.

"I do. But I won't interfere unless there's trouble. Keep your phone volume up, so I can warn you if anything comes your way."

"Okay, but we plan to stay in public."

"Good idea."

Aunt Elise dropped me off a short walk down the road from the restaurant, so she wouldn't "cramp my style." I wasn't sure what that meant, but it seemed like an important human concern, so I went along with it. The walk was pleasant. The sun had already gone down and the decorative streetlights lining the road provided an intimate glow that conveyed warmth despite the cold wind that blew along the sidewalk.

Brigid stepped away from the wall by the restaurant's entrance and waved to me. I smiled as I approached. She wore a bright red coat that reached to her knees, her hair pouring over it like a black waterfall. The red shirt I wanted would have complemented her outfit.

"Wow! You cleaned up good!" she said. "But still the ponytail? I was hoping to see you put your hair down."

"That wouldn't be me," I replied.

"Too bad. I bet you'd look dashing."

I grinned. "Shall we go in?"

"Whatever you want." She walked ahead of me toward the door, a slight spring in her step that made her hair bounce.

I stepped in front and opened the door for her. I wasn't completely new to human culture. I have watched enough movies to know basic chivalry.

My cell phone vibrated in my pocket and played a musical chime. But it wasn't a phone call, so I left it there and followed my date into the building.

Fratelloni's wasn't a fancy, expensive restaurant, but it wasn't a cheap pizza place, either. It was somewhere in between, with good food at a reasonable price and a warm atmosphere. As with all the businesses on this strip, the outer walls of the building were made of brick, but were dominated by a large picture window overlooking the sidewalk we had recently vacated. The dining room was small and intimate, but with tables expertly placed to enhance the atmosphere while providing plenty of seating. As with most restaurants, the lighting was dim and warm.

"Good evening," said the host as we entered. "Table for two?"

"Yes," I said with a slight bow.

"Something in a quiet corner," Brigid cut in with a wink.

"Of course." The host took two menus and led us toward the back. My cell phone made that noise again. I wondered absently what it could mean.

The table was indeed in a quiet corner. We were by ourselves near a staff door to the kitchen. I held a chair out for Brigid, then settled into a seat across from her. It gave me a good view of the rest of the dining room, as well as the big window at the far end, in case the vampire couple came in.

We took our menus and began reading.

"What's good here?" Brigid asked as she flipped casually through the menu's pages.

"I've never eaten here, but I like Penne Al Forno."

Brigid nodded. "That sounds delicious. I'll have that."

I ordered, both of us getting the same dish, and handed the waitress our menus.

"So, Malcus Molova . . ." Brigid sat with her elbows resting on the table and her hands woven together with interlaced fingers. She leaned forward and rested her chin on those fingers, and smiled playfully at me. "Why did you decide to ask me out?"

I was taken aback by the question, but recovered quickly. I considered it for a moment before replying. "You kept sitting with me in the cafeteria, and I wanted to get to know you better."

"And that's it?"

"Well," I said, and I felt my face heat up. "That and you're pretty."

I needed to relieve myself of the awkwardness of her questions, so I countered with one of my own. "Why did you choose to sit with me in the first place?"

"You're new, and you're interesting. And you're handsome," she added with a grin. She did *not* blush.

"You could be with any boy in school. I've seen how the boys in Gym class are."

"But none of them are Malcus Molova, the fascinating boy with the strange name and adorable ponytail."

Our drinks came. One Coke for me and an iced tea for her.

Brigid took a sip from her glass, then set it down. "You said you smelled danger in town. That got me curious. What danger do you smell?"

Once again, I felt uncomfortable with her questions. It wasn't that I didn't trust her, but that they touched on subjects I was unwilling to answer. But I didn't want to say "no." I was trying to make a good impression, after all.

"Well, I never said I *smelled* anything," I said with a smile. "But, well, it's hard for me to say what the danger is exactly. I've seen and heard things that make me think some dangerous people are here in town."

"Ah, the seedy underbelly of Durbin Point. What kind of danger? Organized crime? Murder?"

I exhaled, and her smile faltered slightly. "Murder, if you must ask."

My cell phone made the noise again, which made Brigid frown.

"Someone's sending you texts."

"What? What are 'texts'?"

She looked at me sidelong. "Are you serious?"

"Yes. I've only recently gotten a cell phone."

"But everyone knows what texts are, even those without phones."

"I've been out of touch for a while."

"I'll say so! They're small written messages sent from cell phone to cell phone. Take your phone out."

I pulled it from my pocket and unlocked it.

"There should be an icon that looks like an envelope—probably at the bottom of the screen," Brigid said, taking a tone like Mrs. Pearson from school.

"I see it." It brought up an app that had one name on it: "Elise Petran." The number three was on it inside a red circle.

"Oh! It's my aunt. I think she sent me three texts."

Brigid smiled. "Tap her name and they'll come up."

"Thanks." I wondered what Aunt Elise was trying to tell me. It must have been urgent if she had sent three. I tapped her name and the three short messages appeared.

The first said, "Call me right away." It was dated 6:58, right about the time I met Brigid.

"Call me now. It's urgent!" read the second one.

I stared at the final text. Brigid was talking to me, but I couldn't hear her, the import of the message taking all of my attention.

"Your date is a monster!"

"What's wrong?"

It was Brigid. Her words broke through the shock of Aunt Elise's text. I looked up at my date and stared at her. Her expression was soft, her delicate features wrinkled in concern.

"Are you okay?" she said.

I had suspected that she was a monster, but Aunt Elise had

allayed my fears. Now she told me I was right. But Brigid looked like a normal girl. Well, prettier than a normal girl, but still within human possibility.

She waved her hand before my face. I jumped and shook my head, as though to clear it.

"Sorry," I said.

"Was it bad news?"

I glanced at my phone, then back to her.

"Kind of. Unexpected is more like it."

"Does it have to do with that danger you've been talking about?"

"I think so. Maybe. I need to send a text. Please bear with me."

"Of course." She seemed sincere.

I typed quickly on my phone, *What kibf?* I hit the send button too quickly, so I sent another that said simply, *kind?* I wasn't certain I would ever get used to using such a small device.

"I hope she's not in trouble."

"Huh? Who?"

Brigid motioned toward the phone. "Your aunt."

"Oh! Yeah. No, she's fine. I'm sorry for being a rude date."

"It's good. You straighten that out, and we'll get on with it."

"Thank you."

Another message came. *I don't know. Be careful.*

Well, that was it. I was on a date with an unknown type of monster. It couldn't be a coincidence that she became interested in me. She knew I was a sorcerer, or at least mythic. I decided to go for full disclosure. It would be safer to do it here in public, rather than outside, where she could fight me.

I set my phone down as the food arrived. The dish smelled

delicious. She gently stabbed a piece of chicken that rested on a bed of penne and put it in her mouth. She smiled as she chewed.

"Very good!" she said.

I took a bite of my food, then washed it down with Coke.

"Where are you from, originally?"

"Ireland," she said.

I nodded. "Are you a banshee? I never pictured them being so pretty. A fairy, maybe?"

Her eyes narrowed suspiciously. "What are you getting at?"

"You're a mons—a *mythic* person. I'd like to know what kind."

It was her turn to feel uncomfortable. She frowned and stared hard at me.

"So you're a sorcerer? And your parents—investigators, you say. They must be in the Alliance."

"And you are . . . ?"

Brigid let out a long breath, this one laden with trepidation. It is amazing how many reasons once could sigh for. "I'll tell you. But I want you to know that I'm a good person. I had no idea you were mythic. I've been telling you the truth all this time."

She paused. "I'm a dhampir."

My knowledge of dhampirs was limited. I knew they were the children of a vampire and a human, where the father was a vampire and the mother was human. They're supposed to have some, or all, of the powers of a vampire without any of the downsides, like burning up in the sun. I had no idea if dhampirs were always evil, like their fathers.

I looked at Brigid with my Magic Sight. She was full of energy, having more than a typical human. I also got the distinct impression the energy was hers, and not stolen from someone else, but I couldn't be sure.

"Say something," she said. She sounded worried, almost sad. "Please."

"You don't look like a vampire. I mean, on the *inside*. You have your own energy, like all other living things."

"Well, that's good to know. What else does your X-ray vision tell you?"

"That you like to tell jokes."

She smiled. "It's a defensive mechanism. I crack jokes when I get scared or nervous."

"You've never looked nervous until now. But you joke a lot."

"It relaxes me."

"You're nervous around me? Why?"

"Isn't it obvious?" She paused, as though she assumed it was. "Because you're cute!"

"But you have an easy time with boys. They fawn all over you."

"And I *hate* that. I think it's part of my dhampirism, and I can't help it. But it doesn't seem to affect you. I like that."

"Interesting," I said. I must admit, it answered a lot of the questions I had about her.

"Do I pass the test?" she asked. Her voice shook slightly as she spoke, but her face did a good job of covering it. "Do we have to fight to the death, or can we enjoy our meal?"

"I'd rather not fight you to the death. Between the two, enjoying our date would be my preference. But I have a question. Do you kill people?"

"No. And I don't drink blood. I don't have that affliction, so I can live happily with humans. Which I do."

"Good. That's a big help. I have a problem with cold-blooded killers."

"So do I. Now are we good?"

I smiled. "For tonight, at least. This took me by surprise. You must understand, I can't say everything is awesome. I'll need to do some research and some thinking. But as long as you're a good person and not a killer, I don't see any problems. I'm not against dating mythic people. That would be hypocritical of me, don't you think?"

She grinned. "Yes, it would. And if your aunt wants to meet me, that's okay."

"Good. I'll text her to let her know we're fine for now."

I texted Aunt Elise. *Learned some things. Tell you later. Finishing date.*

Dinner conversation left the interrogation behind, and we had a good time talking about the challenges of living in the human world. Apparently, she had spent many years living with them, so she felt less awkward than I did.

"So, you don't have any parents." I set my napkin down and leaned back. "How can you be in school without any?"

"I live with a couple that are essentially foster parents. It's a long story, but they know what I am and they help me out."

"Sounds like there's a story behind that."

"And you'll hear it, eventually. We need to have topics for other nights." She winked at me.

After dinner, we went for a walk, just back and forth on the downtown strip. The air was crisp and the ocean breezes always managed to reach us, but it was nice. We even held hands as we walked. I was glad to feel that her hand was nice and warm, as it should be.

"Now that you know what I am," Brigid said as we walked. "Can you tell me about this danger? It's supernatural, right?"

I nodded. "There are vampires in town."

"I know. They live in a house on Harrison Street. The abandoned one."

I flashed her a look. "How many of them?"

"Only two. They've been trying to play it cool, hunting in other towns and stuff. I've been watching them and waiting for a chance to strike."

"You would fight them?" I asked.

"Of course. I hate vampires!" At my confused look, she sighed again. "I'm not one of them. The truth is, they tend to hate dhampirs with a passion. They think we're unclean." Her laugh was packed with irony. "I think they're envious, because *they're* the dirty ones."

"Well, those two are dead," I said.

"They are? When?"

"I killed one a few days ago, when it attacked me in the woods. I killed the other today, in that house." I decided not to bring Oni into the story. At least, not until I'd verified that Brigid was safe.

She paused as she considered the news. "Then that's it. The danger's gone."

"I'm afraid not. There's more of them." I told her of my encounter the other night, and I described the two vampires.

"I've seen them." Her voice was flat, expressionless.

"Clearly, you have something against vampires."

"You're going to kill them. These vampires." It wasn't a

question.

I nodded. "That's the plan."

"Why? Why do you do it? You're just a kid."

I looked at her askance. "As are you . . ."

"Yes," she said quickly. "But I need to know why you do this."

"The Alliance declared open season on vampires decades ago. They're a threat we can't fully eradicate, so we do what we can to keep their numbers down."

She stopped walking and turned to me, locking my gaze with those sumptuous brown eyes.

"That explains your parents. But why do *you* do it?"

I shrugged. "Vampires killed my grandfather."

"Was he close to you?"

"Very."

"Good. You won't succeed in killing them if you aren't properly motivated. I'll help you."

"And what's your motivation?"

Her piercing gaze softened, and tears wet her eyes. She looked away.

"I *had* a brother and a sister. Now I have no one."

"We're trying to find their lair. We thought there was a pack, but the two I killed seem isolated."

Brigid began walking again, her hand still clutching mine. "You said you think there's a pack. What's your evidence?"

"I have none. Usually, if there's more than one, there's a pack."

"I never knew about these new ones. If they can hide from me, that suggests a pack."

I saw Aunt Elise's car. I stopped walking.

"I think our date's over. I see my ride." She glanced around, then noticed Aunt Elise's car.

She smiled at me. "Okay. I had a good time. I honestly did. It might have had its rocky moments, but it's so good to have someone I can *really* talk to. Now I know you're not just a pretty face."

"It *was* nice," I said. "But sometimes I wish we could talk about normal things."

"Then another date, after we kill the pack."

"That sounds good," I said. "But should you be the one asking?"

"I didn't want to wait for you to get around to it."

We stood there for a moment and looked at each other. It might sound sappy, but we looked into each other's eyes. Then, before I knew it, we were kissing, and it was everything I could have hoped a kiss would be.

Chapter Twelve

"She's a *what?*" Aunt Elise almost slammed on the brakes as she navigated the darkened streets of Durbin Point.

"A dhampir. I know what you're thinking . . ."

"How *can* you know what I'm thinking and still continue your date with her?"

"She's not a vampire, Aunt Elise."

"She's a type of one. And she has all of their benefits and none of their weaknesses."

"Yeah, like drinking blood. She eats like we do and has no urge to kill humans. She might be related to vampires, but that distinction makes her more like us."

"Brigid told you this? How can you believe her? *She's* the monster!"

"I used Magic Sight. All of her energy was hers. None was stolen."

"All of it?" Aunt Elise showed doubt for the first time that night.

"All of it. And she eats regular food, too. I watched her

down a whole dish of pasta."

Aunt Elise frowned. "A vampire that doesn't drink blood. I didn't know such a thing existed."

"They aren't turned, like vamps are. They're born this way. She grew up a dhampir."

Elise pulled into the driveway. She turned the engine off, then looked at me.

"Do you like her?"

Did I? The girl was more than pretty. I enjoyed our conversations, and I found the prospect of having a friend, or *girlfriend*, who was also mythic refreshing. "I do."

Aunt Elise sighed. "Then I won't forbid you from seeing her. At least not yet. I have some research to do on dhampirs. You must understand that if what I discover is dangerous in any way, I might have to forbid you from seeing her."

I climbed out of the car. "Aunt Elise," I closed the door and leveled her with a hard gaze across the Camry's roof. "I don't like being lied to, especially by a monster. If she turns out to be a serious threat, I won't want to see her!"

I walked with Aunt Elise to the house and waited as she unlocked the front door.

"This town is a lot less mundane than you thought," I said.

She snorted. "Tell me about it."

"Well, with the vampire pack and now a dhampir, I thought—"

"I didn't mean *literally*!" she snapped.

Ah, a human figure of speech. Now that I have friends, I should learn more of those.

Once inside the house, Aunt Elise relaxed. She locked the door, then put the pot on for tea. She leaned against the counter beside the stove and her tension lessened noticeably.

"I'm not ready for this." There was a quiet desperation in her tone that I had never heard from her before.

"Not all monsters are bad," I said.

"But how do we tell? I mean, vampires, they're easy. But this dhampir. I don't know."

"You have contacts. Talk to them. They'll help you."

She went to the cupboard and pulled down two mugs. "Of course, you're right. I'll make some calls tomorrow. But please be careful with that girl until you know better. For all we know, she might not even be a girl."

"Aunt Elise, I know she's a girl. Trust me."

She chuckled, but it lacked humor. "I mean, she might not be a *kid*. Vampires don't die. They stop growing once they turn and live forever until killed."

"Brigid was born a dhampir. She was never turned. That means she was a dhampir as a baby. I doubt she stops growing."

"But we don't know, and that scares me."

"Well, we'll have to do some research and learn."

The teapot whistled. Aunt Elise pulled it off the burner and filled both mugs. She handed one to me and took the other for herself. Her face clouded over as she lost herself in thought.

"I think I'll go upstairs and do some research," I said.

She nodded as she stared absently across the room, her mug suspended below her lip.

I went upstairs to my room and closed the door. Even with all the talk about Brigid being a dhampir, I still found myself preoccupied by one thing: that kiss.

It was the first time I had ever kissed a girl, and I must admit, it was far more exhilarating than I had imagined. Now, I understood why humans put so much thought into it. So many songs have been written about kisses, and books and movies, too. It all made sense. I wanted to talk about it to someone, to tell them what it was like. But even more, I wanted to kiss her again. Brigid was a mythic person, and that was important, but all I could think about as I sat at the bay window and looked out at the night scene below was if kissing a human girl was as good. I thought about Kathy but dismissed the idea outright. She talked far too much, and I didn't find that attractive, even though she was cute. Tracy, however, was intriguing. She dressed all in black, like me, and she didn't talk much. But her smile, when she did smile, was pretty. Yes, I could see myself kissing Tracy. But not now. Right now, there was only one person I wanted to kiss, and she wasn't human. I guess that experiment would have to wait.

I shook my head, then took a sip of tea. I needed to get that kiss out of my mind. It was a distraction. And I had research to do. I went to the computer and turned it on. I had no books with me on monsters, so I had to depend on the Internet for my information.

I wondered if *A Sorcerer's Guide to Magic, Monsters, and the Mythic World* would have anything on dhampirs. I wondered if they were known to have superhuman kissing abilities. *No, of course not!*

I turned on the computer and browsed to the website. The *Guide* came up, and I clicked in the search box and typed "dhampir." The screen refreshed and a new page appeared. It had the same background picture as the page on vampires. That didn't fill me with confidence. It meant the *Guide* considered them to be monsters. The text appeared shortly after, and I began reading.

The dhampir is the child of a male vampire and a female human. Female vampires cannot have children, so a dhampir always has a human mother. Not much is said in human mythology, and human literature has expanded on the concept, but they tend to stray far from the truth.

The dhampir is dangerous, having most of the vampire's abilities and few of its weaknesses. For instance, it has heightened strength, more than is humanly possible, but less than that of a vampire. They are also fast, capable of sudden bursts of extreme speed, but again not as swiftly as a fully fed vampire, although some are trained to be more agile. Dhampirs do not have the ability to daze their victims, but they can manipulate the emotions of humans and weaker-willed mythic people. They have great healing capabilities, and don't age as quickly as humans do once they reach adolescence.

There are two types of dhampir. This Guide calls them dhampir monsters and dhampir people. Dhampir monsters are more like vampires in their personality and behavior, whereas dhampir people are more like sorcerers in temperament and intelligence. It can be hard to tell them apart until it's too late. It's not certain how a dhampir becomes a monster or a person, but the current theory has to do with the mother. If the mother dies during childbirth, the dhampir born will probably be a monster. If the mother survives, then the child is likely to grow up a dhampir person. We think it has to do with nurturing. If the dhampir is never properly nurtured when young, it's likely to not have the bond that makes them see others as more than prey.

Dhampir monsters are extremely dangerous, since they aren't as limited as vampires. They are wolves in sheep's clothing, as they live among humans and prey on them, as well.

Dhampir people are like other people: some are good, and some are bad, while most are somewhere in between. Dhampir people should be treated like any other mythic person, with respect and the benefit of the doubt. Unfortunately, many sorcerers don't see it that way, and treat all dhampirs as monsters.

Dhampirs have no special weaknesses. They can be killed like most other people, but their heightened healing and other abilities make it difficult. Still, they are vulnerable to most weapons, if they stay still long enough for someone to get a shot at them.

I sat back from the computer. With as much information as the article had, it failed to answer my biggest question about Brigid, and left me with even more. She could be a monster or a mythic person. I still didn't know if she was a danger to me.

They can manipulate emotions. Brigid said she couldn't help it. Was she lying? Was our kiss just an attempt to manipulate me? Would it even work on a sorcerer? A vampire's daze didn't, so it seemed likely that wouldn't either.

Did her mother die when she was born? She implied that vampires killed her family. I suppose she could blame her mother's death on vampires if she had died giving birth to Brigid. But how could she have brothers and sisters if her mother had died?

I had to find out, and I had to do it discreetly, to make sure she didn't lie. For the first time, I understood the benefit of being ignorant of the mythic world, like humans are.

Sunday dawned clear and cool. As much as I wanted to deal

with Brigid, I had more pressing matters to attend to. The vampire pack was out there, and I had to locate its nest. And that meant I had to go hunting. Tonight, I planned to hang out downtown and see if those two vamps showed themselves. If I stopped them from feeding the other night, then they might be more desperate. This meant I'd be more likely to find them. It also meant they might attack someone, and I would either have to make myself known or let them kill.

I did my homework during the day, then helped Aunt Elise around the house. We decorated for Halloween, carving pumpkins for the front porch and hanging decorations. That was fun, and I came to understand some of humanity's interest in such a *supernatural* day. Most humans don't believe in Halloween, but nearly everyone celebrates it. They took an important and serious night like Halloween and turned it into a fun family holiday. I thought that was fascinating.

When night came, I prepared for my outing. Aunt Elise wanted to join me, but I talked her out of it.

"I know you're worried about me. I'm still young. But you can't fight them, and are you prepared to let them hunt for the sake of finding their nest?"

She frowned. "No. Are you?"

I shrugged. "I certainly hope so, or there could be trouble."

"I wish I could talk you out of this. It's so dangerous. But I know it must happen. If we don't destroy the nest, this town is doomed."

"That's right," I said. "I'll be okay. I know what I'm doing."

"Be careful."

"I will. I can always teleport home if I get in trouble."

The sky remained clear that night. The moon, large in the

sky, glowed brightly, casting a silvery sheen over the streets. My walk downtown was more pleasant than before. I felt more at ease now that I understood what was going on and was prepared to deal with it. The people I passed as I made my way downtown were normal, even using Magic Sight.

At first, I wandered up and down the street, enjoying the cool air and the scents of fall. The decorative trees that lined the sidewalks had turned to magnificent reds and oranges and yellows. The air held the scent of wood fires, and the warm glow of the street lights mingled with the moon to create the perfect backdrop for a walk around town. After three circuits along the downtown strip, I decided to buy a tea at the coffee shop and take a seat on one of the benches. I sat alone, sipping tea and pretending to read a book. I smiled pleasantly as people passed by, but so far, none were the two vampires from before.

I yawned. With all that had happened in the last few nights, I found myself getting tired, and I was painfully aware that I had an early morning tomorrow for school. I didn't know how much longer I could stand the inactivity.

A couple walked past, and I looked up, my pleasant smile already on my face, and then I started.

It was the vampires!

Her skin was flush with color, while his skin tone had diminished some since I saw him last. She had fed, and recently. They hadn't noticed me, so I remained seated until they were nearly out of sight. Then, I stuffed my book in the backpack I carried, and followed them at a discreet distance. My Magic Sight enabled me to see them from a greater distance, so I was certain they didn't notice me as they walked leisurely down the road.

They left the downtown strip and made their way toward the coast. The couple showed no sign of hunting. There was nobody in front of them, and they chatted amiably as they walked, the woman hanging lovingly off the man's arm.

They were heading home! The woman had already fed and now they were walking back to their nest. I was torn. On the one hand, I was glad that they were returning to their lair, but on the other I was appalled that she had already killed. I tried not to think about that.

I pulled out my phone and texted Aunt Elise about my discovery. Now that I understood texting, I found it to be a useful tool.

We continued our walk down Main Street, which ended at the junction of North Shore Road. We had traveled three blocks and were only one block away from the junction.

A blur of something shot from across the road. Then the woman was gone, leaving the man to stagger backward as if he had been pushed. The tall, burly vampire looked around in shock, then turned his attention to the side yard between two properties. With a growl, he charged across the front yard of the home to disappear behind a fence that separated the two yards.

I was dumbfounded by the sudden turn of events. I couldn't imagine what had caused the woman to vanish like that, but I had to find out.

I ran as fast as I could toward the house where the commotion had occurred. When I reached the end of the fence, I peered around it.

A small strip of yard, no more than eight feet wide, ran beside the house to give access to the backyard. The vampire woman lay on the grass, motionless, several gashes on her neck and body. The larger vampire stood beside her, squaring off against another monster.

It was Brigid!

Her face hadn't transformed, like vampires faces did when they attacked, but there was something animalistic about her features. She stood semi-crouched with her hands held out before her like claws. In the dim moonlight, it looked as though they *were* claws.

The vampire charged Brigid, and to my sight, it seemed like he teleported to where she was. One second he stood beside his lover, tensed to spring, and the next, he was where Brigid was. But the dhampir had moved. In a quick blur of motion, she dodged to the side, her clawed hand having raked his face, judging by the cuts on his cheek once he stopped moving.

I realized what I faced with that pack. The two monsters I had fought before were nothing compared to these stronger and more experienced vampires.

I also felt certain that Brigid was out of her league. The male vampire seemed unfazed by Brigid's counter-attack and prepared for another lunge. The female vamp was now stirring. Brigid had two strong vampires to contend with. I had to think of something quickly, or the girl I kissed last night was going to die.

The big vampire charged once more, this time catching Brigid before she could move, and the two of them slammed into the wall of the house. If I had hit that house that hard, most of the bones in my body would have shattered. The two wrestled with each other, both striving to deliver a fatal blow.

I worked magic, and I worked it feverishly, hoping to get it right quickly enough to save Brigid's life.

A light came on in the second-floor window above the two combatants, and the window opened.

"GET OUT OF MY YARD!" shouted a man's voice from the window. "I've called 911! The police are coming!"

The reaction from the combatants was instantaneous. The male vampire, who had grabbed Brigid by her throat and raised a hand to finish her off, instead threw her with such strength that she might have been a rag doll. Then he ran and vanished from view.

The woman ran off as well, but slower, traveling only as a fast human.

I ran to Brigid. The light and window reverted back to normal as I released my illusion.

"Are you okay?" I asked as she pulled herself into a sitting position. She glanced at the window and then at me.

"That was you?"

I shrugged. "I had to do something."

She glared at me. "I had it under control."

"Not from where I stood."

Brigid shook her head. "You know nothing about me. I was fine."

"You might be right about that. But what were you thinking going after those two?"

"They're vampires," she said, venom dripping off every word. "I *kill* vampires." Those last words came through clenched teeth, and I noticed she was still in her monster form. Her fingers were indeed like claws and she was breathing heavily. Even her voice sounded husky and vicious. I needed to be careful, to calm her down. But that wasn't how I was thinking.

"We need to find their nest, and you just attacked the only

two vampires we know of," I said reprovingly. "We'll *never* get them to show us where the pack sleeps now."

"And thanks to you, they got away and will warn the rest that a dhampir is hunting them. Their whole pack will be after me."

I had opened my mouth to retort, but nothing came out. I paused as the import of her words sank in.

"Instead of chasing them away, you should have helped me fight them. I could have gotten the location of their nest from them."

"You're right," I said at last. "I should have helped fight. I hadn't thought of that. I'm sorry."

Brigid-monster glared at me. Although her face had not transformed, there was nothing beautiful about her expression. In fact, I was gripped with a sudden terror, as though she might bury those claws into my neck. But then she changed. She stopped panting as she calmed down. Her claws retracted into her hands. And her expression softened. Brigid-monster had gone, and only Brigid Talog, the girl I dated, remained. And she was hurt. I saw blood on her. I think her head was banged up, and her shoulder, but there might have been more injuries. She took a beating.

"Are you okay?" I said again as she slumped into my arms.

She grimaced at the pain but nodded. "I'll be fine. I just need to get home."

I helped her get back to her house. The walk was slow, but easy. Brigid could walk on her own, but my help eased her pain and allowed us to move more quickly.

"Couldn't you teleport us or something?" she asked as we hobbled along.

"I don't know your place. We could go back to my bedroom, but I suspect that would be inappropriate."

She smiled despite the pain. "Just maybe."

"Are you sure you don't need a doctor?"

"How do you think a doctor would react to me?"

"Oh, that's right. You're not human."

"But we dhampirs can heal just about anything. I'll be okay."

"Do you think you'll be safe at your home?" I asked.

"Tonight, yes. They'll take the time to protect their lair. Then they'll hunt for me. It's only a matter of time before they find where I live. And I can't fight a whole pack."

"Then we'll have to get them first," I said.

Brigid sighed. "You didn't do wrong back there. You had told me about them, so this was your battle, not mine. I shouldn't have gone after them without discussing it with you first."

"Well, this time, we'll work together. With your fighting abilities and my magic, we can make a good team."

"Okay. I won't go rogue anymore. I'll play on your team like a good little girl."

I grinned. "That's better."

"Here's me," she said, stopping and gesturing toward a small house. It was like the kind that's rented out to vacationers who want a beach-front property for the summer. Although there was no beach, the house, being on the southern end of North Shore Road, provided a great view of the ocean.

I frowned. "A lot of windows. Not very defensible."

"I wasn't planning to defend myself when I got it."

"You live here alone?"

"Everyone I know is dead."

"I guess I thought you'd be in a foster family, or something."

She chuckled. "That would be funny. Now, I should go in and rest. I'll be fine from here on." She shed my arm's support and turned to face me.

"Thanks for helping me out. Maybe we could have done better, but probably not, since we weren't working together. Again, that's my fault." She leaned forward and kissed me.

Fireworks went off in my head, and I wondered if she was messing with my mind again. It would not be for the last time.

Chapter Thirteen

Aunt Elise was disappointed that I had failed to find the nest. I didn't tell her about the fight with Brigid. I didn't think that would help Brigid's case with her. I told her that someone distracted me and I lost them.

"You'll be trying again, then?" she asked.

"Of course," I said, even though I wasn't sure anymore. "But not right away. I don't want to look obvious."

I texted Oni while riding the bus to school. I told him I saw the vampires again but lost them before they got to their lair. I decided not to tell him about Brigid being mythic.

"Tracy's a vampire!" Kathy said as soon as we were all together at our team table.

"What?" Oni and I said in unison.

Kathy laughed cheerily. "For Halloween! She's dressing as a vampire. *Totally* works, right?"

Tracy shrugged. "I'm still trying to decide between that or a zombie."

"You're still trick or treating?" Oni said as he pulled his Social Studies book from his backpack.

"No. But there's the dance . . ."

"A dance?" I asked, confused.

Kathy gasped, then looked at me. "Could it be, you don't know what dances are?"

"It could," I said, a smile tugging at my lip as Kathy beamed at the news.

"Well, where do I begin?" she said. "Here in America, we have dances at school. It's an event the school puts on in the gym. They decorate the room and have music playing, and the students go to it and dance together."

"We all dance together?" I was still confused.

All three of my friends laughed.

"No, no, no," Kathy said. "You dance with your date."

"Oh!" I said. "So it's a big social gathering for couples."

"Right!" Kathy said. "But some people come alone. That way, they can meet people."

"And for Halloween, everyone dresses up," Oni said.

I nodded. "Okay. I think I understand." I looked over at Tracy. "I think you shouldn't go as a vampire. They're too cliché." With the real vamps around, I didn't want my friends to dress up as one.

"And zombies aren't?" she said, her voice as monotone as always.

"They're better than vampires."

Tracy shrugged. "Zombie it is."

"Are you going to ask Brigid out?" Kathy asked. "Because if you don't, I'm sure there's another girl you could ask." She glanced sidelong at Tracy.

Did she want me to ask Tracy? Thoughts of my earlier experiment sprang to mind, but I felt certain that Brigid would not appreciate me going to the dance with a different girl.

"I should ask Brigid," I said.

"Okay, but if she can't . . ." Again, the discreet look at Tracy. Tracy rolled her eyes.

"Do you want to go to the dance, Kathy?" Oni's face turned red as he said it and he seemed unsure of whether he should look at her or look away.

Kathy's eyes widened and her unbelievably big smile grew still larger. "I would *love* to, Oni! I'll *totally* go with you."

The two of them then dove into a discussion of what they should dress as for the dance.

Tracy and I exchanged wry grins.

"So much for getting work done," I said. She nodded.

Halloween decorations had been set up all around the school, but although I hadn't noticed the posters for the dance when I came to school, I couldn't avoid them after my friends had told me about it. Apparently, the dance was not free, and I would have to buy a ticket for myself, and presumably for my date. I decided it was important that I ask Brigid at lunch that day.

I saw one of Mark's friends in the hallway as I was on my way to Math class. He ignored me as we passed each other, although I was certain he had noticed me.

Oni was all smiles at lunch. He told me he was surprised he had the courage to ask Kathy to the dance.

"I was so nervous," he said. "But it was worth it."

"I'm glad you're going with her," I said. "She's a nice girl."

"But I can't believe she said that about you and Tracy . . . in *front* of her."

"I have to admit, Tracy is pretty. And she's nice."

Oni looked at me as though I was crazy.

"You're dating the hottest girl in school. Why would you even think of asking anyone else?"

I shrugged. "I didn't say I was. I just said she's cute."

Oni gave me a suspicious look. "You can't fool me, Malcus."

"Okay, I thought about it, but I won't. I like Brigid."

"That's more like it," Oni said, a satisfied grin playing on his face. "You're starting to turn into a normal kid."

"Oh, I hope not!"

We both laughed as Brigid joined us.

"What did I miss?" She looked from one face to the other.

"Nothing," Oni said after a final chuckle. "Boy stuff. You wouldn't want to know."

"I see."

"Well, that's my cue," Oni said, standing up. "Nothing personal, Brigid. I thought I'd give you two a chance to make googly eyes in peace."

"You're too kind," she replied with a smile. "But you're always welcome to join us."

"Thanks! Maybe another time. Malcus wants to ask you stuff." With a wink at me, he turned and zoomed away, dodging people on his way to dispose of his lunch tray.

Brigid flashed me a quizzical look, her head tilted a little. "Ask away!"

I laughed, then smiled at the pretty dhampir. "Would you care to accompany me to the dance on Friday?"

She smiled, and I felt I could stare at it for years without blinking.

"I would love to, of course. But I can't."

I frowned. "Why not?"

"Because of last night. I need to keep a low profile. Until we go after the nest, I have to be hard to find. I came to school today so that I could tell you. But after school, I'm leaving town for a while. We can keep in touch by phone, and plan our attack. That means you'll be on your own to find the nest."

I shook my head. "Oni knows, so he'll help."

"You told *him*? And he believed you?"

"Remember the first vampire I killed in town? It attacked Oni. Now he knows. He's been helping me."

"But he's vulnerable to them. Their daze."

"I gave him a charm that protects against that. It worked, too. He staked the second vamp."

"Really?" She considered that for a moment. "I'll never look at him the same again. Does he know about me . . . what I am?"

I shook my head. "Didn't know if you'd mind."

"If he's going to help us fight these things, he should know."

"All right. I'll tell him."

An awkward silence followed.

"No dance, then?" I said at last.

"You should go. I bet you've never been to one."

"I haven't. But I can't go without you."

"Yes, you can," Brigid said. "And you *will*. Consider it part of your study of mundanes."

My brow furrowed in a mixture of confusion and consternation. "I will not ask another girl to the dance."

"And you had better not!" Brigid said, but she grinned as she spoke.

"Now I'm confused," I said. None of this conversation made any sense to me. "According to my research, boys are supposed to ask girls to the dance. How can I go without you if I don't ask another girl?"

Her grin, which had been playful until this point, suddenly softened.

"Not all boys bring a date to a dance. A lot of them go alone or with friends. The same is true for girls. Many boys hope to meet girls there. But you won't, right?"

"Of course not. But that begs the question: why should I go if not to dance with a girl?"

"To listen to music. To spend time with friends. To study mundanes at a social event."

She had a point. It was a research assignment. "You're right. There's a lot to learn there. I think I *will* go to the dance."

Chapter Fourteen

Oni came over to my house after school. We had a Math exam coming up, so we decided to study together. Aunt Elise fed us snacks as we worked at the kitchen table. We were both good at mathematics, so studying didn't take long. When we had finished, we went upstairs to talk.

"Where could the vampires be living?" Oni said as soon as we had settled in my bedroom.

"You're still thinking about that?"

"I never stopped. I've been attacked twice. I won't stop thinking about them until they're all dead."

I nodded but said nothing.

"Something's been bothering me," Oni began, staring down at the floor, his brow creased with concern. "When we find their lair and it's time to go and kill them, it'll be just us. Only you and me, right? I mean, it sounds like your aunt isn't up for doing battle."

"Right. She doesn't have the power or the skills. But I'm

glad you brought that up. There's something I have to tell you."

Oni's gaze shifted from the floor to my face, but his look of concern didn't change.

"We're not alone in the fight. This might be hard to believe, but Brigid is a mythic person, too."

He stared at me, unblinking.

"Am I the only human in this town?"

I chuckled. "It's starting to feel that way."

"What is she? A sorcerer like you?"

"No. She's a dhampir."

"That sounds something like *vampire*."

"That's because they're related. But a dhampir is not necessarily evil. They don't drink blood, and they don't need to hunt people. But they have many of their abilities."

"She's not afraid of daylight."

"No. But she's strong and powerful and hates vampires as much as we do. Maybe more."

Oni paused to let it all sink in. "I know you like her and all, but she sounds a lot like a monster. How do you know we can trust her?"

"Her entire family was killed by vampires. She'll help us."

"But what about after, when all the vamps are dead? How do we know she won't turn on us?"

"Because she lives in your world."

"Murderers live in my world. Those *vampires* live in my world."

I grimaced. "Point taken."

I glanced at my computer and then went to it. I switched it on, brought up my browser and clicked on the bookmark.

"I'm going to show you something. I think you'll find this

useful."

The window cleared and the familiar page of *A Sorcerer's Guide to Magic, Monsters, and the Mythic World* appeared before us.

"I'm still not certain as to how accurate this site is, but so far it's been spot on."

Oni joined me at the computer. "There's a website about your world?"

"Apparently. I only recently discovered it."

I did a search on the site for *dhampir*. When it displayed, I pushed my chair back from the desk to give Oni room.

"Read it."

Oni read the page.

"This doesn't help much," he said at last. "According to this, she could be a monster or a person."

"But it says that if she's a monster, she'll behave more like a vampire. I know how to identify vampires based on their behavior, and Brigid doesn't act like them. She's not a hunter, and she doesn't size up everyone she sees as prey. She's a mythic person, I'm sure of it."

Oni sighed. "Okay. Fine. I'm sorry if I sound a bit paranoid, but all this is hard for me to swallow, and it's made me view my world as a lot more dangerous than I ever imagined. I can't walk down the street anymore without suspecting everyone I pass of being a monster."

"I understand. But we can trust Brigid. She's one of us."

"Okay. I trust *you*, and if you trust her, then that's enough for me."

"Good. Now, before I lost them, the two vampires were walking down Main Street toward North Shore Road."

"Right." Oni thought. "There's not much out there. There's the boardwalk, which is closed this time of year. But that would only make a temporary home."

"What about the arcade? Hardly anyone is there, even when it's open. I thought it didn't make sense when I was there. Maybe that's why."

"Are you saying the arcade's run by vampires?"

"They can have servants. Humans that they feed off without killing. When a vampire drinks some of your blood, they also inject a sort of venom into your system. It doesn't hurt you, but it sort of makes you addicted to their bite. Packs have been known to use humans this way to protect their nests."

"The arcade is run by vampires?" Oni chuckled dryly. "I can see that, but it sounds like a cheap movie."

I flashed Oni a quizzical look. "Inexpensive movies have plots like this?"

Oni laughed, deep and loud. "Oh, that's classic!" he said at last. "No. A cheap movie is a bad one made on a small budget. The stories are usually pretty lame."

"Ah, I see. Do you think a lame story would be less likely to be true?"

My friend chuckled some more, shaking his head slowly. "No. You could be right. I think we should check it out."

"It'll have to be this weekend. The sun goes down early these days."

Wednesday after dinner, Aunt Elise and I went shopping. I needed to pick up items with which to build a costume. Aunt Elise suggested Count Dracula as a fitting costume.

"I told my friends not to dress as vampires," I said.

"Why? Because of the real ones? I don't think it matters."

"Still, it's what I said."

"Don't worry about it. I think you'd make a perfect Dracula. Besides, a little mockery of your enemy will be good for your morale."

I hadn't thought of that. I had to admit, the idea of making fun of vampires sounded good. "Okay," I said at last.

We went to a department store in the next town over for most of the shopping, but eventually made our way to downtown Durbin Point. Evening had set in and the streetlights came on to illuminate the picturesque street scene. I sat outside on a bench while my aunt stood in line at the coffee shop. I started a conversation with Brigid on my phone via text.

"Found any leads?" she asked. I had assumed she would ask about the upcoming dance, but she dove straight into the topic of vampires.

"No. The vamps were heading toward the shore, so we think the arcade is a possibility."

There was a pause. "Not likely. Isn't it still open?"

I typed the answer as quickly as I could. Oni had showed me how to use my thumbs for typing, and I was gradually growing competent at it. "Yes, but only barely. I always wondered why a place like that would stay open with only a few customers."

Another pause. "Be brief with texts. Drop unnecessary words."

I frowned. "I like to be correct."

"But it's a lot of typing."

"I don't mind." I smiled as I hit the send button.

"I thought you wanted to fit in?"

"Not if it means dumbing down my vocabulary :)." Oni taught me the "smiley face," as he called it. He told me I shouldn't use a period with it, but I had to end the sentence.

"A period. Seriously?" came her reply. It appeared she also didn't approve.

"Do people ignore punctuation in texts?"

"Hello there." I jumped, as my attention had been completely held by my digital conversation. The woman vampire had taken a seat beside me. She wore black yoga pants with nothing covering them and a black fleece jacket. She had left the jacket unzipped and her shirt underneath exposed more of her chest than was appropriate. I forced my eyes uncomfortably to her face, but her smile was also overly provocative. Do all adult women flirt with teenagers, or only the vampire ones?

"Hi," I said, turning my gaze toward the coffee shop. I could see Aunt Elise through the picture window. Three people stood in line before her.

"You spend a lot of time here by yourself," the woman said. "That's not normal."

"I like the cold air and the dark," I said.

"Again, not normal."

"You're alone tonight," I said. She talked as though she remembered me, so I decided not to play dumb.

"I'm not married," she replied. Her voice took a somewhat husky tone, which was oddly arousing.

I looked at her again, partly because of her voice change and partly because of what she said. I hadn't asked her if she was married. She had a beautiful face. Black hair fell in gentle curls over one eye, leaving the other brown eye to send a shiver up my spine. The skin of her face looked soft and fair. It was paler than last time I saw her, so she hadn't fed since then, but she shouldn't be hungry enough to hunt.

I decided her statement meant that she was available for dating. "I'm a teenager," I said.

"And that matters?" Again that smile. It drew me in. I wanted to kiss her. Ever since I kissed Brigid, I've wanted to kiss girls. I've kissed a dhampir. I thought about kissing Tracy. But a *vampire?*

I shook my head and looked away.

"How are things with that boy you fought?" she said, changing the subject.

I released my breath. It seemed an appropriate time and wouldn't give away my anxiety. I welcomed the change of subject. It was less awkward.

"We're good."

"I like you. You have a certain style that intrigues me. I don't want that boy to hurt you."

"He won't. We've made up."

She shook her head and looked at me as though I were an innocent child. "Men like that prey on the weak. And, I'm sorry to say, you are weak."

"Mark respects me for standing up to him."

"All the more reason why he'll hurt you again. You stood up to him in front of his followers. He can't let that go unpunished."

"He punished me. You were there."

"That wasn't enough. This Mark . . . his minions won't approve of leaving you alone. They'll want more, and he'll have to give it."

"Are you sure?" I asked.

"I'm certain. You need to get strong. I can make you strong. Come with me, and I will ensure you will never be a victim again."

"Really? Will you teach me Karate, or something?"

She chuckled, and even that was alluring. Although vampires had no hypnotic powers, and they were not inhumanly beautiful, this woman was quite capable of manipulating men with her body.

"I can show you. It's not far."

I had an opportunity. Here was a vampire offering to show me her lair. But it was most certainly a trap. She intended to feed on me, make me one of her junkie slaves, or turn me into a vampire. The things she said implied the latter. If I went with her, I'd be forced into a fight, and I didn't trust my odds.

I glanced over at the coffee shop. One person was ahead of my aunt.

Are human children taught to mistrust strangers? I hoped so.

"I'm not supposed to go anywhere with strangers."

Her smile widened. "But we're not strangers. We're friends. I was on your side at the fight. And you want to come. I can tell."

"I don't even know your name," I said.

"Isabella. And you are?"

"Malcus."

"See? We're friends now. Come with me, and I'll show you things you could only imagine."

She stood and held her hand out to me.

I did my best to look torn. "I can't. I'm sorry. Maybe another time." I glanced at Aunt Elise. She was paying for her coffee.

The woman followed my glance, then nodded.

"Another time then. But I'm holding you to it."

"Okay."

"Bye-bye." She waved to me with her fingers, then turned and strutted down Main Street.

I was still staring at Isabella when Aunt Elise arrived with her steaming cup.

"Someone I should know about?"

I looked up at her and smiled. "Oh, nobody special. Just a vampire trying to be friends."

The surprise on her face was magnificent!

Chapter Fifteen

"I'm so glad you two are going out!" Kathy exclaimed in Social Studies the next day.

"They're not *going out*, Kathy," Oni said carefully. "It's only a dance, and we're all going together."

"I refuse to believe it's not a date." Kathy said this to me with complete confidence. "You two like each other, and that's awesome!"

"But I told Brigid that I wouldn't be taking a date to the dance," I said. Kathy said nothing for once, but she winked and then fell into a fit of giggles.

I glanced at Tracy. She flashed the hint of a smirk she often displayed when Kathy did something cute. I chuckled.

Tracy's next subject was in the same hallway as mine, so we walked together. We didn't talk at first, which I attributed mainly to Tracy's quiet nature. I decided to break the silence.

"I'm looking forward to the dance," I said tentatively.

"Even though you're not going with Brigid?" Her tone was

flat, no hint of jealousy audible, aside from the context of her words.

"Well, *yeah!*"

She flashed me a quizzical look.

"I like Brigid. I really do." Words streamed unbidden from my mouth as though I needed to say them. "But I like you, too. It's confusing . . ."

That was it. My mouth ran out of words, and I trailed off. Tracy looked at me in her emotionless way for a moment, then smirked.

"It's only a dance, Malcus. It's not a big deal. We're all going as friends."

We walked on in silence after that, Tracy looking ahead while I stole furtive glances at her. She always kept her expressions blank, hiding her feelings from everyone, but there was something about her face at that moment that I found curious. A hint of pink accented her usually pale cheeks, betraying some emotion. I tried to interpret the signs but found her inscrutable. Color to her cheeks could mean she was blushing, but it could also mean she was annoyed or frustrated.

Humans.

Aunt Elise helped me create my costume for the dance after school. I didn't understand why humans dressed up for Halloween. It seemed an odd custom, but apparently it was observed in many nations around the world.

"I believe it started with the day's real properties," Aunt Elise explained as she made adjustments to the coat we had bought. "You and I both know that on Halloween, the spirit world and our world are the closest to each other as they will ever be. In the old days, people used to dress up as the dead to celebrate. Over time, as people's belief in things like that waned, the custom changed to what it is today."

I frowned. "But people dress up as anything, now. That doesn't make sense."

"The custom has evolved. Take away the mysticism and you're left with people dressing up. It's no longer about the dead."

"Interesting." I decided not to ask about Trick or Treat.

"Tell me about this girl, Tracy. What's she like?"

"Well," I said, grateful for the topic change. "She's human."

Aunt Elise chuckled. "That's a plus. Is she nice?"

"Of course. She dresses all in black and acts serious all the time."

"Ah, the goth. Always quiet and expressionless. Do you want me to explain what a goth is?"

"No," I laughed. "I know what it means. And she expresses herself in interesting ways."

"It sounds as though you really like her. This will be your second date with as many girls. You're becoming quite the Casanova."

"Who?"

Aunt Elise flashed me a warm smile as she worked. "Casanova. A famous Italian lover from the eighteenth century."

"Ha ha," I said in mock derision.

"Dating more than one girl at a time can be tricky. Just try not to hurt them."

"This isn't a date. Technically, I'm attending the dance with Oni, Tracy, and Kathy."

"But Oni asked Kathy to the dance."

"Yes."

"So, they're on a date. That leaves you and Tracy. I think you two might be going together without you realizing it."

"Oh!" Could she be right? Could it be that this was their plan all along? It sounded pretty devious for two girls to plan that out. I knew, of course, that Oni wouldn't have been involved. He liked me dating Brigid. "I'll be careful, then," I said.

"You said that woman vampire wanted to be friends with you?"

"Yeah, she offered to teach me to be *strong*. I think she wanted to turn me into one of them."

"You're playing a dangerous game talking to her. I don't approve."

"I had no choice. She sat down with me before I knew she was there. If I got up and left, I'd look suspicious. I don't think a teenage human boy would run away from her."

Aunt Elise sighed. "It's dangerous. She was trying to trick you. To manipulate you."

"But I know what she is, so it won't work."

"Would you have gone with her if I wasn't there?"

I thought about it. The temptation to follow her was still fresh in my mind. "No. It was a trap, and I knew it. I'm no fool, Aunt Elise."

She sighed. "I know you're not, Malcus. Your parents have done a fine job raising you."

"Thank you," I said with a slight bow of my head.

Aunt Elise sat back from her sewing machine and raised the coat. It was black, and with her modifications, the collar raised higher and stiffer than normal. It looked *exactly* like Dracula's coat on the movie poster we looked up.

I grinned.

The day of the dance dawned chilly but clear, with a bright blue sky and wispy white clouds carried by ocean breezes. The school was abuzz with an excitement I could almost feel, like an electrical current that shot from smile to smile as I made my way to Social Studies. The dance was the common subject in hallway conversation.

Kathy was a conductor of that current of excitement. She had dressed up as a cat, with white pants, a fuzzy white sweater, cat ear headband, and whiskers drawn on her face. She even had a fake tail attached to her pants. Her smile was brighter than usual, a feat I hadn't thought possible. She talked non stop about the dance.

The three of us exchanged glances and grinned. Tracy affected a slight tug at the corner of her mouth. The rest of us had reserved our costumes for the dance, so we were dressed normally. Time went by quickly as I focused on our work. It wasn't that I didn't care about what Kathy had to say, but I found it impossible to follow her train of thought.

The rest of my classes also went quickly. Before long, it was lunchtime. Without Brigid in school, we had the table to ourselves.

"I don't know about this dance," Oni said as we ate our lunch. "I'm not a good dancer."

"You seemed pretty graceful fighting that vampire," I said.

"That's my Aikido. It's a graceful art. But I've never danced before."

"Isn't Aikido similar to dancing?"

He thought about that. "I guess so. Kind of. But I don't want to hurt her."

"Maybe you can think of it as you try to dance."

"I guess I can try that. Good idea. Aren't you worried? Do sorcerers ever dance?"

"No, I've never danced before. But my Aunt Elise taught me last night. I think I know what to do now."

"Lucky . . ." he said wistfully.

"Besides, I don't plan to dance with a girl. I'm dating Brigid."

Oni took a sip from his milk. "I think Tracy expects you to dance with her. Kathy's been talking about it. Didn't you hear her in class?"

"To be honest, I couldn't keep up. She said I have to dance with Tracy?"

"She talked like it was expected. You might have to."

"This complicates things. I'll have to make sure she knows we're only friends."

"I'm sure Tracy will understand," said Oni.

"I met one of the vampires the other day," I said and told him about my encounter with Isabella.

"Whoa! That's kind of cool, right?"

"She wanted to turn me into a vampire."

"Oh . . . I guess not then."

"But at least that means she doesn't know I'm mythic, and *that's* good."

"Yup, but if you went with her, you'd know where the lair is."

"And it would become *my* lair."

"True."

"We're still on for the arcade?" Oni asked, downing his carton of milk in one long pull.

"Of course. It's our only lead, right now."

"Good." He rose, put his backpack on, then lifted his tray. "I'll see you at the dance."

Chapter Sixteen

Friday night had come, and I stood in the living room in my costume, Aunt Elise smiling as she examined the ensemble.

"Well?" I asked. I felt awkward. This was the first time I had ever worn a costume. I know now that most people would consider my ritual robes to be a costume, but I never thought of them that way. A costume is something you wear to affect a character who is different from yourself. I'm a sorcerer, so my sorcerer's robes are appropriate. This, however, was not *me*. I wore a black suit with tails and a collar that stuck up longer than it should. I wore a top hat, and I carried a cane. I had plastic caps for four of my teeth to transform them into fangs.

"You look fabulous!" my aunt exclaimed. She pulled out her phone and snapped a picture of me.

"Please promise me you won't show that to my parents."

"I'm making no such promise." She smiled mischievously, and I let her have her fun. She had been under stress from the whole vampire situation, so she was due a little levity.

My friends and I had all exchanged phone numbers. The plan was to text the group when I arrived and we'd all meet up at the dance.

Aunt Elise drove me to the school. It was a chilly October night, but the rain had gone, allowing the fallen leaves to blow in the breezes that always came from the coast.

"Are you sure you don't want me to stay at the dance?" she asked as she navigated the dark side streets that led to Durbin Point High School.

"I'm sure. Vampires aren't going to attack a school dance."

"But this is your first big social event in the human world. It might be overwhelming."

I rolled my eyes. "I know you don't think so, but I'm a big kid. I can handle myself."

She shook her head slowly, but smiled all the same. "I can trust you to handle a vampire or some other monster. But a school dance? That's *different*."

"Funny," I said.

"It's not meant to be. I don't think you understand what you're getting yourself into. Human kids are prepared for events like this. You're not."

"I'll be fine. And I'll have friends with me."

Aunt Elise chuckled. "Then don't be too proud to lean on them if you need help."

"*Really?*" I must admit I whined a little. I'm not proud of it, but Aunt Elise had pushed my buttons, and I couldn't take it any longer.

"Fine," she said calmly. "I'll drop it. But take it easy in there, okay?"

I nodded, choosing not to trust the tone of my reply.

Aunt Elise pulled to a stop behind a line of cars parked beside the walkway. They were all dropping their children off. I opened the door.

"Hey!" my aunt said as I climbed out. "Take it easy. And don't be afraid to call me if you want to come home early."

"Okay," I said simply. I knew I shouldn't be offended by her belief that I would have trouble, but it bothered me.

She smiled. "Have fun!" I closed the door, and she pulled out of line and drove off, her taillights disappearing among the chaos of cars in the parking lot.

I looked at the door. A dozen or so kids in a variety of costumes walked past me to enter the school. I saw two superheroes, a girl in black robes carrying a wand, two boys who looked like walking corpses, and a girl dressed as a princess. No one was dressed as a vampire.

I felt conspicuously out of place. I had thought, when Tracy recommended a vampire, that this was a common costume. But I was the only one there. I was struck by a sudden anxiety. What if this *wasn't* a common costume? What if everyone in the dance hall stared at me? I experienced a reluctance to enter the school that I had not expected.

I took out my phone and sent a text to our group chat. "I'm here."

This gave me the excuse to await a reply. It came right away from Tracy.

"On my way. Let's meet at the snack table."

That would be in the building. I replied with an affirmative, pocketed my phone, and approached the door. It seemed imposing, like a portal to another dimension. I willed myself to reach for the handle, but my arm wouldn't move.

A boy dressed in camouflage fatigues, boots, and helmet sidled past me, opened the door and went through the hydraulics, pulling it slowly closed behind him.

This is ridiculous! I fumed silently. It's the school. I've been through this door dozens of times already, and it never scared me like this, not even on the first day of school. It must be because of the costumes. What else could it be?

A girl came up beside me. She was dressed as a fairy, complete with butterfly wings. She smiled at me as she opened the door. She stepped in, then held it open for me.

It was now or never. I had to go through with her holding the door for me. I nodded my thanks, took a deep breath, and walked past her and into the main hall.

Many students loitered there, each in their own costume. A few of them looked my way, but none of them seemed disapproving of my persona. Bolstered by their acceptance, I made my way to the gymnasium.

Music blared throughout the room, making it difficult to think. Streamers and decorations hung everywhere, with a banner above the stage that read "Halloween Dance." Fake skeletons were set up along the walls. Colored lights flashed from all angles, adding to the chaos of the music and people.

People.

Easily a hundred students were in the gym, either dancing in the center of the great room, or congregating in small groups along the walls. It was like Roger's Arcade, only ten times worse. The music was far too loud, and that alone made me hesitate to enter the gym.

I like quiet. Nice, calm places that are neat and orderly. I can't perform magic in that bedlam. Not that I planned to, mind you, but I always felt a need to be *able* to. Like a lion bearing its belly to a stranger, I would be making myself vulnerable, and that terrified me.

Two girls walked past me, yelling at each other to be heard over the racket. They marched headlong into the chaos of the gym as if it were any other room. They were completely unaffected by the noise and lights and crowd.

I had to get over this. Like at the front door, this was a hurdle, and I had to face my fears to get beyond it. Again, I took a deep breath, then plunged into the din.

I moved slowly through the crowd, making my way awkwardly across the dance floor to the refreshment table that stood against one wall. I passed people whose mouths were moving in conversation, but I heard nothing from them in the pandemonium. I reached the snack table and stood nearby as I awaited my date.

How can they do this? I thought, holding my hands to my ears. *Don't they know this will damage their eardrums?*

Someone tapped me on the shoulder, and I jumped. Oni stood next to me wearing a Karate uniform, Kathy at his side in a cheerleader's outfit. She waved. He said something I couldn't catch.

I pulled my hands from my ears and shouted.

"WHAT?"

"WHERE'S TRACY?"

"SHE'S COMING. NOT HERE YET."

"IT'S GREAT, ISN'T IT?" Kathy shouted.

I shrugged. "IT'S TOO LOUD."

Oni laughed. "YOU WOULD HATE A ROCK CONCERT!"

I stared at him blankly. A *rock* concert?

He laughed again but didn't respond.

"THERE SHE IS!" Kathy shouted, and we all looked across the room.

Tracy stood framed in the doorway. She wore a long black dress that almost covered her black shoes. A long wig hung straight and black over her shoulders. Her face looked pale, and she wore black lipstick.

"MORTICIA ADDAMS!" Kathy shouted with glee. I surmised that was the name of Tracy's character, probably from some movie or television show.

Tracy made her way toward us. I was pleasantly surprised to see that she appeared annoyed by the noise and the crowd as well. Of course, she always kept her expression blank, but she showed her disapproval in subtle ways. It was mostly with her eyes, as she rolled them when a new song started, and they darted to a couple that danced a little too energetically, forcing her to go around them.

"WOULD YOU LIKE A DRINK?" I asked her when she joined us at the snack table.

She glanced at the table, and I saw a slight twitch of her lip. Then she shook her head.

"LET'S ALL DANCE!" Kathy said. She nudged me, then motioned toward Tracy.

I ignored the motion. Kathy had been treating this dance as if Tracy and I were going as a couple, but we had both set her straight on that. Still, Kathy kept trying to force us together. Tracy and I exchanged a glance, and she rolled her eyes. I grinned. Then we followed our friends to the dance floor.

Aunt Elise had spent a few evenings teaching me how to

dance. Apparently, she was young enough to be knowledgeable of current dance techniques, as I was able to move to the music in much the same manner as the others, with only a few modifications. Kathy and Oni laughed a lot, and I smiled. Tracy rarely smiled, but she showed her enjoyment through her body language. She was loosening up a little. We danced for a while, bouncing and moving to the easy beats of songs that seemed custom made for dancing.

The song changed, and it was a slow ballad. I wasn't sure what to do. Though my aunt had prepared me for this type of dance, I suddenly felt that I should not do this with Tracy. I doubted Brigid would approve. Tracy seemed to understand because she nodded toward the snack table.

With our heads closer and the music quieter, we were able to talk without shouting too loud. I took advantage of the opportunity to make conversation.

"Are you enjoying the dance?" I asked.

"It's fine. You?"

"I like being here with you and the others, but it's too loud."

"I don't like the music."

"We could go for a walk. You know, in the hallways."

"Okay."

We finished the dance, but when the song changed back to a loud one, I took her hand and led her gratefully out of the gym and into the hallway. We walked aimlessly down dimly lit corridors in silence for a while. The music was reduced to a dull thumping beat that came muffled through the walls.

"You don't like that music?" I said, making conversation. "What kind do you like."

"Lacuna Coil, Paradise Lost, The Cure. Bands like that."

"What are they like?"

"Dark."

I smiled. Of course they would be.

"May I ask why you always dress in dark tones and hide your emotions?"

She stopped walking. Her mouth twitched at a corner and she looked away.

"You don't have to answer that. I was being too forward."

"It's okay," she said. She paused for a long moment, her eyes staring at the wall.

"I've had a rough life."

"Has it been *that* bad?"

"I was taken from my parents because . . ." she paused. This was hard for her, but she said it was okay to talk about it, so I remained silent, waiting. "Because they were *bad.*"

I frowned. I wasn't sure what she meant by that, but I chose not to press it. "So who do you live with now?"

"My grandparents."

"Are they bad?"

She sighed. "No. But they're old, and they don't know how to deal with me. They're not helpful."

"Oh, okay." I still couldn't understand how her experiences could cause her current behavior, but I never went through what she did, so there must have been good reasons.

"It sounds like your life is improving. And you've got a good friend in Kathy."

The hint of a smile appeared briefly on Tracy's face. "I like her. She makes me laugh."

"I've never seen you laugh."

She put her hand to her chest. "In here."

"Ah!" I said. "And you've got Oni and me. I won't let anything bad happen to you."

"My knight in shining armor."

I chuckled. "That's me."

She squeezed my hand. "I like you."

"I like you, too."

We looked into each other's eyes and moved closer. Then Brigid's face appeared in my head, and I took a step back.

"Let's go outside," she said. "I need some air."

"Okay." We walked toward the front entrance in silence. I could feel her emotional wall go back up between us, and I was certain I had crossed a line. I don't even know why I leaned in like that. I have a girlfriend.

We went out the front door and walked slowly up the sidewalk surrounding the building. I was well aware that we were outside at night, but I was sure there would be no vampires hunting children at a school dance.

"I'm sorry," she said. "I'm just not ready for . . . *that*. I'm kind of complex."

"I hadn't noticed." She looked up at me, and I smiled. That wry grin returned, and relief flooded through me. We were good.

"Well, look who's here."

I whirled around at the sound of that voice.

Mark stood there in all his brutish glory. But this time, it didn't look as though things were square between us. The scowl that contorted his face made his intentions clear. He wanted to hurt me. *Badly*.

With a fist raised, he advanced on me.

Chapter Seventeen

"Come on, Mark," I said, stepping backward as he approached. "We've been through this. You said we were good."

"The hulk of a kid said nothing, but was suddenly on me, his fists pounding with astounding ferocity on my face, stomach, and chest.

I could hear Tracy's screams as Mark savaged me. I fell to the ground, and he kicked me, over and over. I wanted desperately to use my magic but couldn't with witnesses around. No matter what I did to show that the fight was over, he continued to kick me. My nose was bleeding, and I think he bruised at least one rib. I had to do something . . .

Mark stopped abruptly. One second he was there kicking me, and the next he was gone. I risked a peek through the shield of my arms and saw my attacker wrestling with the male vampire who had accompanied Isabella. The vampire beat Mark almost senseless, then sent the bully running.

Someone was at my side, helping me into a sitting position. I was about to thank Tracy when I looked up into Isabella's beautiful face.

"Are you all right?" she asked, her exquisite features creased with concern.

I tried to nod, but that hurt. She put a handkerchief to my nose, and I pinched my nostrils closed, the cloth absorbing most of the blood.

"I know you don't want to hear this," she said softly. "But I was right. That boy will always trouble you until you learn to beat him. I can help you be strong." She nodded toward her lover. "*We* can." The big vampire gave a curt nod.

"Come with us. We can heal you. We can make you strong. You won't be a victim anymore."

Of course, I knew better. But I was afraid they would take over where Mark left off if I refused. I wasn't sure what I could say to handle the situation, so I pretended to be stunned by my injuries. In truth, not much pretending was required. I sat there and looked confusedly at her.

She released a resigned breath. "Think about it. I'll find you when you've recovered from this, and then we can talk."

I nodded slightly, and Isabella motioned for her friend to leave.

I saw Tracy running toward us with several teachers. Of course. She went to get help.

Isabella stood up as the teachers joined us. One of the teachers knelt in front of me and examined my injuries.

"A bigger kid was beating this poor boy. He ran off when I yelled at him."

"We've called the police," said a teacher. "They'll find him."

An ambulance came for me. I resisted. The last thing I wanted was to go to a hospital where they could discover things about me that shouldn't be. I insisted on calling my aunt as we waited for the ambulance to arrive. She raced to the school, showing up as I struggled to keep the medics from putting me in their truck.

"I'm fine, honestly. It's just some bruises. It's not that bad."

"What's going on here?" Aunt Elise said, arriving on the scene.

She dove into a conversation with the emergency medical techs and finally let them bandage me up and then leave me to her. They bandaged my nose and my chest and put my left arm in a sling, then helped me into Aunt Elise's car.

Tracy, Oni, and Kathy hung around the entire time and came to the car window as Aunt Elise got in the driver's seat.

"Thanks for the dance, Malcus," Tracy said. "I hope you'll be okay."

"I will. It's not that bad." I glanced down at my arm, then laughed. Then I stopped because it hurt.

"You get better, okay?" Oni said. "Call me when you can."

"Of course."

They stepped back to let us go. Tracy hesitated, concern etched on her face. I grinned and waved, and she joined the others.

Aunt Elise drove away. I told her what had happened.

"I'm afraid the vampires have gotten to Mark," she said when I had finished my story. "It sounds like they turned him into one of their slaves."

"Really? Just to convince me to go with them? That seems extreme."

She pulled the car into our driveway and turned off the ignition. "He's big and strong. They would also use him as a guard and as food."

Aunt Elise helped me into the house and up to my bed. She examined my nose and my arm, and then took off my shirt and examined my ribs.

"Hmm," she said. "It looks like I've got my work cut out for me. You rest here, and I'll take care of you." She kissed my forehead, which was the only part of my body that didn't hurt, and left.

Before long, I could smell food cooking downstairs. She came up shortly and fed me more of a pound cake she had made before, then she prepared a ritual.

Aunt Elise had power, after all. But she apparently specialized in medical magic. I realized then, as she cast her spells over me, that her cooking had some powerful recuperative magic in it. She had been using her powers around me the entire time, and I never knew it. She was truly amazing.

Two hours later, she turned out the light in my room and left me to sleep. I didn't think I would be able to, with the night's events racing through my mind, but she must have given me a sleeping draught or something, because I fell asleep right away.

When I awoke the next morning, I discovered that my arm was no longer broken, although it was still sore. My ribs were completely healed, as was my nose, which had not been broken in the first place. All the bruises were gone.

"You'll have to pretend to be hurt," she said at breakfast. "And a glamour to recreate your bruises would be a good idea."

"How come you never told me about your magical skills?" I asked.

She shrugged. "You never asked. I wasn't trying to hide them. Weren't you aware that your wounds were healing quickly?"

"Yes, but I never realized it was because of you. But what you did last night was amazing."

"Why thank you, Malcus." She bowed, then served me breakfast.

I looked down at my dish. "Is there magic in this?"

"There is a little magic in everything I do."

I took a bite of egg. "I have a question, though. How were you able to convince the medics to let me go with you?"

"Because they thought I was a doctor." She took a seat across from me and nibbled a slice of toast.

"You are full of surprises."

She smiled, and we ate in silence for some time.

At last, she turned her gaze to me, taking a sip of tea. "What's your plan for today?"

"Oni and I are investigating the arcade."

"Ah, going to play some games. Good idea. You need the time off."

"But we think it might be hiding the pack."

Aunt Elise frowned. "Are you sure?"

"No. But it's a place to start."

"You were just beaten up by one of their guards. What's to say it won't happen again?"

I swallowed a bite of bacon and grinned. "I couldn't use magic then. I can there. If I need magic, it'll be in private where it's safe to use."

She considered that. "I suppose you're right. You know, your parents will be proud of you when I tell them what you've accomplished."

Chapter Eighteen

It was nine o'clock in the morning when I left the house to meet with Oni. I was well-rested, fully recovered from last night's ordeal, and ready for action. The great ball of the sun hung above the horizon like a bright beacon, guiding me to my destiny at the end of Dunmore Street.

But I was premature in those thoughts. The monsters were still around, hiding in their dark prison as they awaited their own destiny.

I emerged onto North Shore Road and crossed it to the seawall. Oni waved to me from farther down the street. He sat on the wall across from the arcade. I walked purposefully to join him. We looked at the dark, dingy building that was built into the strip of boardwalk businesses. I had to admit, if any business was owned and operated by vampires, it would be Roger's Arcade. Having no front facade, it was a veritable hole in the wall. No lights were lit inside, as they would interfere with the myriad computer screens that glowed and flashed ominously from within.

"Are you ready?" I said.

Oni patted his backpack. "Stakes."

"Good."

"You look terrible." Oni's look of concern surprised me. Then I let out a breath in realization. The bandages and fake bruises I had donned before leaving had done their job.

"It's an act. Aunt Elise cured me. This is all for show."

"All of it?" he said in awe. "Dude, that's cool!"

"Let's go!" And I set out across the street, Oni right behind me.

Mark's gang was conspicuously absent from the entrance, and only a handful of kids were inside playing games. Still, the lights and sounds were as distracting as ever.

We worked our way to the back of the arcade, where we saw the counter. It was a long, glass affair with prizes on display to be purchased with tickets dispensed by some of the games. A fat man with a surly attitude sat on a stool behind the counter. A door to the back rooms was behind him.

"How are we going to get back there?" Oni asked.

I shrugged. "A distraction?"

"But what?"

At that moment, a young boy approached the counter.

"Sir, Q-Bert took my money."

"What do you want me to do?" the surly man, who I guessed to be Roger, the establishment's namesake, snapped back.

"Get me my money."

Roger growled, then said "all right." He reached down and grabbed a toolbox and followed the kid to the game, muttering as they went.

Oni and I exchanged glances, then ran behind the counter, opened the door, and slipped through.

If I thought the main arcade room looked dark, dingy, and eerie, the hallway we found ourselves in was ten times worse. Old wood-paneled walls painted gray framed the narrow passage that extended in both directions to the end of the business's part of the strip. The floor was uneven and creaked as we walked toward the end.

There were three doors along this passage. The first opened into a small bathroom. I gagged at the stench that assaulted my nose when Oni opened the door. But the odor was normal public-toilet reek. A lot of it. No smell of rot or desiccation.

The second door opened into a somewhat large room filled with broken arcade machines, tools, and cleaning equipment that I doubted saw much use. We searched the room for trap doors and hidden entrances but found nothing.

The last door was locked.

"You can't magically pick a lock, can you?" Oni asked.

"I could, but I don't think I need to. I'll leave my body for a minute, and I'll be right back." I closed my eyes and concentrated. I looked inside myself and pictured my essence being something different from my body; something vital and alive inside my physical form. I then moved outside of myself. My astral form, which was invisible to Oni, walked through the door into the third room.

It was an office. Small Brad cramped, it had an old wooden desk with a computer and telephone. A heavily worn office chair behind the desk was the only other furniture in the room. The place was not much larger than the bathroom we had seen, and smelled only marginally better. I searched the room for other exits, but there were none. Disappointed, I went through the door and back into the hallway, then stopped in stunned silence.

Oni and my body were gone.

The hallway was empty. My body was nowhere in sight. I couldn't keep this up for long. If I didn't reenter my body in the next minute or two, I would be trapped in astral form forever.

I strode through the wall into the arcade. I ran to the aisle near the counter and looked down it.

There they were. The fat owner had both Oni and my body by the upper arm and was leading them roughly toward the exit. My body, still alive and with the memory of the soul that had left it, stumbled along like a zombie.

I ran down the aisle as fast as I could and jumped into my body just as Roger gave us a shove out onto the boardwalk.

". . . and I don't want to see you kids around here ever again! Got that!"

"Yes, sir!" Oni said, a hint of fear and guilt in his tone.

Roger turned and stormed back into his domain, leaving us outside on the boardwalk.

Oni turned, grabbed me and shook me roughly. "Malcus, snap out of it!"

I pulled away from his grip. "Cut it out! I'm here. What happened?"

"The guy caught us in the hallway. He kicked us out and told us to never come back."

I shrugged. "I'm fine with that."

"Did you look into the room?"

"I did one better. I left my body and went in. It was a normal office. No secrets. The arcade is another dead end."

Oni stared at me for a moment. "How can you talk casually about something like that?"

I shrugged.

"Hey, Molova!" The voice was loud and bassy, as though it came from someone big and strong—probably with a thick neck and few brains.

I froze.

Oni whirled about and assumed the same loose stance he had taken with the vampire he fought.

"What do you want?" he challenged. He was either brave or stupid, I wasn't sure which.

"We want to talk with Malcus. It's about Mark."

Something about those words and the tone of voice used to say them brought me out of my shock. I turned to face the newcomers. It was Mark's gang of friends.

"What about him?" I asked.

One of the brutes motioned across the street to the seawall. "Let's go over there, where we can talk in private."

I nodded, and we all crossed the street. Oni and I kept our distance, to play it safe.

The guy who seemed to be in charge cleared his throat.

"I hear Mark went after you last night. Did that." He motioned to my fake injuries.

"First, I'd like to know who I'm talking to."

His face crumpled into a confused look, as though I had broken his train of thought.

"Your name is Jake?" I said. "Jake who?"

"Oh! Jake Brogno."

I nodded. "Okay then. Yes, he did attack me."

"That's not like him. He was good with you. He'd finished and was done. There was no way he would have gone after you again, unless you provoked him."

"Which I did not," I assured him.

"Thought so."

"Do you have any theories as to what's wrong with him?" I asked.

He nodded. "He's hanging with a new group. We've seen them before, but we kept our distance. We're tough, but we're not that bad. These guys are nasty."

"I think I know who you mean. A woman is one of them. Black hair, pretty."

Nate snorted and stepped up beside his friend. "She's not just one of them. She's their leader and is the worst. I don't know what their deal is, but there's something not right about 'em. And Mark, well, he's turned his back on us and joined them."

"And you're jealous?" Oni asked.

Jake flashed my friend a threatening glance. Oni winced.

"We're worried about him. He's our friend, and there's something wrong with him. We've watched them. They treat him like dirt, like he's their *slave*. And he does whatever they say, without a single word."

I nodded. Aunt Elise was right. They'd taken him.

"You talked to the leader," Pete said from behind Nate. "We watched you last night. You know something about them."

Nate nodded. "Yeah, tell us!"

These guys had just given me a lot of information. Now they wanted some. It was time to form an alliance.

"Before I tell you, I need clarification on something. You said Isabella's their leader. How many of them are there?"

"I don't know, for sure. But there are four, at least."

"Right. Thank you. These people are bad news. I mean, *really* bad news. If you go after them, they will kill you. Every one of you, and you wouldn't stand a chance. Do you know where their lair is?"

"Lair? You mean their base? Sure. But what are you going to do? If we can't fight them, how could you?"

I smiled. "I can't, of course. But I know people who can. The proper authorities, so to speak. Tell me where they are, and we'll get Mark back."

Jake turned and looked at his friends. They all nodded.

"Okay. They're out there." He pointed at the island that was barely visible from where we stood but was not far from shore. It was near the Dunmore Street intersection.

"There are at least four of them and two goons, including Mark." I said.

"No. There are more goons than that, but I don't know how many."

"All right. I'll tell my contacts and they'll take care of the situation."

"Nope. That's not how it's going down. We came to you for information. Now we'll do the fighting. It's our friend."

"I hate to say this, but these people—those four ringleaders. They're more dangerous than you think. Mark is essentially their slave. You saw that. You don't know what you're dealing with, and you're unprepared for it."

"Then prepare us!" Nate shouted. "Unless your *contacts* are the blasted Marines, you'll need us."

"You just don't understand." My voice was heavy with frustration. They didn't get it, and I didn't think they ever would. But I had to convince them to back down.

"Hey, Malcus." It was Oni. I looked at him as though I'd forgotten he was there. Which I had.

"What?"

"I think we should let them help," he said.

"Yeah!" shouted Pete. Jake and Nate nodded their agreement.

"But you know what's going on? How can we let them in on it? They won't believe it and, therefore, they'll be vulnerable."

"They could take out the guards." Oni's voice was calm, professional. He was confident. "We might be able to stop four—you-know-whats—but when you add the guards, we're really outnumbered."

I closed my eyes and rubbed them. It wasn't because they bothered me. It helped clear my thoughts.

"Fine! You can help. But you have to do what I say. Leave the ringleaders to us. You take care of the others."

Jake shook his head. "We'll rescue Mark."

"He's probably one of the guards now. And if you only focus on freeing your friend, you'll fail. Everything depends on the ringleaders going down, and that can't happen if my comrades and I can't get to them."

"How do you plan on fighting four grown people?" asked Pete. "You got some extra muscles hidden your coat?"

"Honestly?" My respect for them, which had been rising during this conversation, took an immediate dip. "We have our intelligence, skills, and tools. We know what we're dealing with, and we know what to do to stop them."

Jake looked at me suspiciously. "Why don't you tell us? Just say the words 'These ringleaders are dangerous because they . . .'"

"Are vampires!" finished Oni.

I flashed him a angry look. "Oni!"

He ignored me and scowled at Jake. "What did you think we'd tell you? These are people smart enough to ensnare the minds of others. Obviously, they have some drug they're using and Mark fell victim to it. All those guards did. Do you want to end up like your friend, or are you willing to let us do what we do?"

"If we knew everything you do, then we can help more," Jake said. It was hard saying no to him when he made such good sense. Under normal circumstances, I'd say he had a right know. I suppose he probably did now. But I couldn't tell him the truth.

"I wish I could. Honestly, I do. But you have to trust us. I can make sure the ringleaders are stopped, but I need you three to knock out or capture the guards. Can you do that? If Mark is with the guards, you can knock them all out and take your friend away.

"All right, all right. So, you won't tell us. Yeah, we'll deal with the guards and Mark and leave the rest to you. It's your funeral. But the problem is: we don't know how many of them there are or what they're doing on that island."

"Then I guess I'll do some reconnaissance," I said.

"I'll come," said Jake.

"Nope. Just me. I'm small and nimble and can move silently. Can you?"

He let out a frustrated breath. "Whatever. When will do you it?"

"Tonight. Right before dark. It won't take me long."

"Good. Meet us at Durbin House of Pizza once you're done. We'll make plans then."

He spun abruptly around and strode off, his two friends following behind.

I turned to Oni. "You don't happen to know how to row a boat, do you?"

My friend grinned.

Chapter Nineteen

It was a half-hour before sundown, and icy water of the Atlantic came in lazy waves to make the small rowboat bob beside the pier. This was a narrow dock stretching out from the seawall to a point unaffected by the tide.

"Are you sure you can manage this?" I asked Oni, who grinned and hopped into the craft. It looked awfully vulnerable in the surf.

"Come on!" Oni said, when I hesitated. "You need to do this, and this boat is all we have. I can handle it. I've used it tons of times."

"Very well." I climbed carefully in, painfully aware of how cold the ocean water was. Oni said it was like that all year round. But the iciness of it almost hurt when a small wave hit my fingers that clutched the gunwale.

"Untie the line, please," Oni said calmly. He was in position, with an oar in each hand and his back to the bow.

I climbed to the front and undid the knot that kept us from

drifting. I gave the pier a slight push, then sat down, dropping the rope to the floor at my feet. Oni took over, turning the boat around and rowing over the waves and away from the dock.

He seemed adept at sea, and we sliced neatly through the water toward the island that grew gradually before us. The rowing got easier as we went farther from shore as the surf wasn't as bad.

"It's called Gaff Island," said Oni as he worked the oars. "There used to be a small watch house there for the military to keep a lookout for enemies, but that was ages ago. I've heard there are ruins of the place still there, but that's it. Nobody uses the place anymore. It's pretty barren and usually covered with seagulls and their crap."

"The building's not intact, then?" I asked.

My friend shook his head.

"There must be some shelter, though. The vampires will need to be in total darkness during the day."

"I don't know what that would be. There's not much there. It's small, mostly barren. You'll see."

The island approached with every stroke of the oars, and I now had a better view of it. What I had initially mistaken for trees were really bare bushes that covered most of the place. It was rocky and had nowhere to hide that I could make out from my vantage.

"I think Jake and his friends were wrong," I said.

"I was skeptical," said Oni with a grunt, as he continued working the boat. "But it was the only lead we had. Look for a place to come ashore."

"We're not going ashore," I said.

"What? How can you search the island from the boat?"

"I can't. But remember the arcade?"

"Oh!" my friend said as understanding struck him. "You're leaving your body again."

"It's the safest way. I want to watch them leave their hiding place so that I can know right where it is. I don't want them seeing me."

"So, I'll get us close but stay offshore. Is there anything else I should do?"

"You should probably stay on the ocean side of the island because the vamps are likely to go ashore."

"Right." He turned the boat to approach from the southeast.

"And don't let me fall in," I said. "My body won't be under my control. It'll be as though I'm asleep."

"Gotcha! Don't be seen and keep you from drowning."

We were now only twenty feet from away from land, and I nodded to myself. "This is good. I'm going to astral project now." I positioned myself off the seat and deeper into the boat so that my body will be less likely to fall in. Then, I concentrated.

The air was warm around me as I traveled across the short stretch of sea to the island. But, it wasn't warm; it was more of a lack of temperature. I existed in a limbo world between life and death and was unaffected by the environment.

Gaff Island was precisely as Oni had described it. Mostly made of rock, the place was uneven with small hills covered in shrubs. They were probably pretty during the spring and summer, but now, they stretched out in all directions with skeletal fingers, as though they reached for my soul as I flew by.

My consciousness soared thirty feet above the ground, moving slowly as I scanned for signs of activity. A motorboat sat tied to the ocean side but at the island's far end. Near it were the ruins. Three of the four outer walls of what was once a stone building still reached upward in a vain attempt to do their job. But they were broken and jagged, adding to the creepiness of the isle with its naked bushes and stark features. The third wall, which faced away from the shore, was gone.

Two men stood inside the old dwelling and looked around. They appeared nervous.

"I hate this part," one of them muttered, and I recognized him as the man who had spied on me.

Bingo!

"Shut up," growled Mark, who was the second man.

Richards chuckled. "Yeah, I was grumpy like that too at first. But you get used to it. You learn to *love* it. Angel is amazing! But you're lucky. You serve Isabella. Now, she's—"

"Shut up!" Mark feigned an attack, and Richards jumped. He might have whimpered.

They stood in silence for a minute as the sun sank lower on the horizon. Then, finally, shadows stretched across the ground, and the inside of the demolished home was bathed in darkness.

"I just hate waiting, is all," Richards said quietly.

Movement caught my attention. The two men stepped away from each other and looked down at the ground. A three-foot square section of the floor inside the old wrecked place shifted and slid aside. Mark kneeled at the edge and helped people climb out. Two men emerged, both strongly muscled and virile. One of them was the man I saw with Isabella. The other had attacked me at Richards's place. Then Angel came out and stood stretching. She arched her back, exposing her beautiful body. Richards stared unabashedly at her chest.

At last, came Isabella, and she took Mark in her arms and kissed him, first on the lips, then on the neck. She held his arm and peeled back the sleeve.

She cast him an exquisite smile, and the brawny young man shuddered in delight. "Just a little nip before I go?"

Mark nodded mutely.

Isabella lifted his arm to her mouth rather than bending her own head to it like Angel had with Richards. Somehow this made her seem stronger, more in control.

I looked away when she bit into him. Angel was doing the same to Richards.

Other men came into the building now. Four of them. Two offered themselves to the men while the others waited their turn. I noticed that Mark was the only teen among them.

Isabella released Mark's arm and licked her lips. "Now run off and take watch, like a good little boy."

Again, Mark said nothing. But he nodded and did as told, jogging out of the ruined watch house and heading toward the edge of the island facing the shore. Angel finished with Richards and sent him to the nearest end.

At that moment, I realized that a guard was bound to be sent to where Oni awaited my return. So I rushed back, flying faster than a seagull across the island and the twenty-foot stretch of water and then into my body.

I gasped and sucked in air.

"Oh, you're back!" said Oni, and he stuffed his phone into his pocket.

"Row!" I whispered. Then I gained complete control and repeated, "Row!" louder. They're coming to guard the shore.

Let's get out of here!"

Oni expertly spun the boat about and rowed away at a strong pace. But I knew there wasn't enough time. So I focused my thoughts on the water and the icy coldness. Mist rose from the surface and engulfed our little boat in the fog. I kept it up until we neared the dock we had come from. Then I released the spell, and our cover began to slowly recede.

Jake and his gang were sitting at a table at the back of the restaurant when Oni and I entered Durbin House of Pizza. The place was well-lit and active. Loud conversations mixed to provide a perfect backdrop to hide our more clandestine discussion. Aunt Elise sat near them with Brigid. They pretended not to notice me, but I caught the hint of a smile break my aunt's facade. Only for a moment, and then it vanished. I had called them as we walked there. They would eavesdrop on our conversation with Mark's friends.

I strode to the group and took a seat, Oni sitting down beside me.

"What did you find?" asked Jake at once.

"Six guards, including Mark. They'll be watching all points along the island's coast. The *ringleaders*," I said, being careful to use the non-Mythic label, "hide during the day in a cellar underneath the ruined building. There's a three-foot-wide hatch hiding the entrance. The leaders will return there by morning."

"How do you know that?" asked Nate.

"I've been watching them. They vanish shortly before dawn and only come out at night."

"Are they vampires or something?" laughed Pete.

"Not a bad analogy," I replied.

"They're just people," said Nate. "Not monsters."

"Some people *are* monsters," said Oni. "And that's what they are. These guys are as close to vampires as humans can get. They took control over Mark's mind, after all." Oni lied a little, but I could understand why he did it, so I left it alone.

Nate opened his mouth to argue, but Jake shushed him with a raised hand. "Okay! We get it. How do we fight them without ending up like Mark?"

"I told you I have connections; people skilled at dealing with villains such as these. They're ready to take action once I fill them in."

"So, you're expecting us to sit back and do nothing?" Jake asked. It sounded less like a question and more like a statement. They were not about to comply.

"It's for the best. My contacts need to work alone."

"Who are they?"

"I can't tell you. They operate in secret."

"I don't believe you." Jake's expression had hardened once I had introduced this fictional group of experts. He only became more skeptical since then. I couldn't say I blamed him. But it was inconvenient as hell.

"Well, you'll have to. You said yourself that these villains are out of your league. I'll see to it that Mark is freed."

I could tell that Jake wanted to refute that, but he only fumed at me for a minute. At last, he seemed resigned to his fate. "Fine! But let me know as soon as it's done!"

"Agreed!"

Jake stood up and walked away without another word. The others followed him out the door.

Aunt Elise and Brigid joined us after the gang had gone.

Brigid smiled, but her typical cheeriness was subdued at the moment.

"I have a bad feeling about those guys," my aunt said. "I don't think your words sat well with them."

"That can't be helped right now. We have to plan. We strike before dawn."

Aunt Elise nodded. "Okay. Let's head home where we can talk in private."

We rode home in tense silence. I sat in the back seat with Brigid and Oni took the front. He stared absently out the window as we drove. Brigid held my hand but seemed lost in thought.

When we arrived at the house, we went in and took seats in the living room. Brigid and I sat on the couch.

"Now that it's come to it," Aunt Elise said. "I'm not comfortable with the plan. We're not strong enough for this."

"But we have no choice," I said. "People are going to die if we don't strike."

"And unfortunately, they've set their sights on you, Malcus. They'll try again to get you, and we can't let that happen. We have no choice but to attack tomorrow, during the day."

"And we're not alone," Oni said. "We have Brigid. She's really tough, right?"

Brigid nodded. I remembered how vicious she was against Isabella and her lover.

"She sure is," I said. Brigid gave me a quick grin.

"So, how many of us are going?" she asked.

"Two," I said. "You and me. Aunt Elise is staying here. She can help us if we come back hurt."

"That's three, Malcus," Oni corrected.

"You're not coming," I said.

"What do you mean I'm not? Of course, I am."

"I'm sorry. It's too dangerous."

Oni's anger rose up, and his face went red. His entire body shook. "That's not fair! I've helped you all this time, and I even killed the last one." Brigid shot me a sidelong glance at this. "I'm not going to be left out. I'll follow on my own if I have to. I will never feel safe here again if I don't see them die with my own eyes."

"You're a teenager, Oni," Aunt Elise said calmly. "And you're only human. These monsters are too dangerous. You have a family. It will break them if you died."

"Malcus is a kid, too, and has a family. Yet he gets to go fight vampires. I have as much reason to do this as he does. I know I don't have magic to use, but I've got his anti-daze charm, and I know Aikido. I'm not without skills."

"If I may interject," Brigid said. "I think we should let him come." When we all gave her strange looks, she continued. "It sounds as though he's skilled enough to help, and he clearly has the motivation. And we *need* him. Four vampires and six guards. This is risky enough with three of us. I don't want to go in with only Malcus having my back. I'm sure he's excellent at what he does, but we need what help we can get."

Aunt Elise frowned. She thought long and hard, then looked from face to face. Finally, she closed her eyes. The breath she released was ragged with defeat, mingled with care.

"Very well. But if I have to attend his funeral, I will never get over it."

"But it's okay if I die?" I meant it as a joke, but my aunt

looked at me, her eyes wet.

"No, Malcus. It's not. I love you like a son, and if you die, *I'll* die inside. But you're a sorcerer, and this is the kind of thing you've been training for. I'm not Oni's guardian. It shouldn't be my choice, but here we are. Oni, I wish we could have modified your memory so you could live a normal life and not take this risk. But I can't, so I have to let you do this."

"All right," Oni said after a pause. "I think we all understand the plan. Kill the vampires and don't die."

We all smiled, but nobody laughed.

"What's the *real* plan?" I said.

Brigid shrugged. "The plan is to show up with the morning sun and take out the guards. Then we open that hatch and force them out into the sunlight. That will kill them."

"And if something goes wrong?" Oni asked.

"We keep them fighting until the sun comes up and then they burn to death. They can't survive the sun."

"What if they don't leave the cellar?"

"We'll have to go down there," I said. "But I'm not worried about that. I can make that cellar inhospitable enough."

Aunt Elise nodded. "To get to the island, you should go by boat. And row, so that you make no sound."

"If we go in the morning," I said. "I could raise a fog on the ocean, to augment any that's already there. They won't see us coming."

"Would that use up too much of your power?" Aunt Elise asked.

I shook my head. "Fog's easy. All the ingredients are there on the water."

"If that's it, we should get a good night's sleep," said Aunt

Elise. "And I have a lot of prep to do in case there are injuries to repair."

"I should go home now," Oni said. "Unless I can sleep over."

"No way," said Aunt Elise. "I'll take you home. But you meet us here at eight o'clock sharp, or they go without you."

"I understand."

Chapter Twenty

Sunday morning dawned cold and wet. It rained in the early hours before sunrise, but had stopped a half hour before we set out. The weather report said the rain was over for the day, but it would remain overcast. This was a good sign, as there would be a lot of fog on the ocean already, and there would still be enough light to keep the vampires locked up. The last thing we wanted was for them to have the run of the island.

Aunt Elise had borrowed a boat from a neighbor. We got it ready by the seawall as the sun's first rays came like a dull blur through the mist blocking the horizon.

Oni arrived on time, so we had no excuse to leave him behind. Besides, Brigid was right. We'd need his help, especially on those guards. His martial arts would come in handy there. Also, he knew how to row a boat, which turned out to be a blessing because neither Brigid nor I had ever done it.

Oni rowed the boat and we sat in silence, our tension mounting we drew nearer the island. The fog was pretty heavy on its own, but I added a little to it, to make sure. I shivered in the cold. The rhythmic *plop* of the oars in the water and the slight grunts of Oni as he raised the oars were offset by the occasional caw of a gull. At last, the dark silhouette of the island rose before us. The boat hit sand, and we climbed out. Brigid pulled the boat up onto shore. I dropped the fog spell, but there was enough natural fog that it made little difference.

The island was small and rocky, the ground a mishmosh of dirt and half-buried stone. Grass mottled with shrubs covered the ground between the stone that peeked through like the bald head of some enormous skulls. The ruins of an old fort dating back to the nineteenth century were supposed to be somewhere on the southeastern end of the island. We guessed the pack would use the ruins as the basis of their lair.

We struck out in that direction, based on the dull blob of sunlight that rose like a beacon behind the mist. The ground was uneven and rocky, and the shrubs had prickers. We dodged those and stepped over loose rocks as we made our way steadily toward the fort.

"Psst!" Brigid stopped moving and held up a hand for caution. We all looked at what had she had found.

A man lay motionless on the ground. He looked pale, as though dead, but it could have been a trick of the foggy light. Brigid knelt and checked for a pulse. She nodded, then rolled up his sleeve and held his arm out. Many puncture holes were visible.

She gently placed his arm by his side. "He's a guard, a slave of the vampires. See the marks? But why is he unconscious?"

We continued on and found five more bodies. All alive. All guard-slaves.

"Someone beat us here," I said, suspicion growing. "I've got a bad feeling about this."

"I know what happened," said Oni. We joined him over by some bushes.

Pete lay unconscious. His arm was bent at an odd angle.

"Jake and company are here. They fought the guards."

"And now we have to rescue them, too," I said.

We crept onward. Oni had a stake in one hand, and his other free. He walked in that loose manner his martial arts training gave him, and his eyes darted around, looking for signs of trouble.

Brigid, on the other hand, was tense, as though preparing to spring at the first opponent to appear.

I had my Force Wall spell prepared. If anything charged me, it would hit an invisible wall, giving me time to cast something more creative.

Forms appeared from the mist ahead of us. I paused, expecting them to lunge at me. But they didn't move. They weren't living figures, but structures. The partial walls of the old fort stood before us, a dim reminder of old wars. I had seen this during my reconnaissance. It was where the vampires lived.

I crouched and made my way carefully to one of the broken walls. It was made of brick and rose up ten feet into the foggy air. But it was narrow, with most of it piled in a heap all around. I knelt behind the cover it provided and waited. The others did the same, finding similar crumbled hunks of wall.

Voices drifted to me from beyond the barrier.

"Are you sure these are all of them?" It was a male voice, deep, bassy, strong.

"Yes." That was Mark. I would recognize that voice anywhere. But it was different. It lacked the confidence and attitude he normally had when he spoke. He sounded weak, as if his will had been broken. "There was only the one boat."

"How can I trust you?" the vampire spat. "You let these intruders pass right by you. We only have one slave to guard us all because of your incompetence."

"Your other slaves weren't strong enough," Mark said, a hint of pride sneaking into his voice.

"I don't care what you say—" began the vampire, but another voice cut him off. The sultry tones covered me like a warm blanket, and I wanted to curl up in it and sleep.

"It doesn't matter now." Isabella's voice sliced through her companion's tirade. "The sun's coming up and we have to get below. I think it's safe to assume we can't sleep today. but at least we can feed. Slave, dump these morsels down the hole, and then take watch."

Mark nodded and turned to comply.

I looked at my friends. Oni was looking at me for a cue. Brigid met my gaze and gave a curt nod. I held up a finger to suggest they wait a moment, then hazarded a peek beyond the wall fragment.

Four vampires stood in a square open area surrounded by more of the crumbled wall. The bodies of three young men lay scattered at their feet. I recognized them as Mark's gang. Jake moaned slightly but didn't move. They hadn't taken my advice and had attempted their own attack. Mark had already grabbed one of them by the ankles and was pulling him toward a trap door near the center of the "room."

I smiled, then cast my Force Wall to lie horizontally over the trap door. Nobody noticed, as the invisible barrier covered their only means of taking shelter from daylight.

I looked at my friends and gave a satisfied nod.

Brigid disappeared in a blur of movement. The big vampire she had fought the other day was thrown back, my dhampir friend on top of him, and her fists pounding into his face.

Isabella turned toward them, standing vulnerable in her surprise. I shot a Force Net at her, which scooped her up and sent her flying against a wall segment. She looked comical, struggling against the invisible webbing that held her in place. I pulled a wooden stake from my bag and ran across the gap toward her.

I had crossed most of the distance when Isabella's eyes locked onto mine. Recognition spread quickly across her face and she stared in shock at me.

Something plowed heavily into me and I fell sprawling on the ground. Twisting around, I found myself face to face with one of the other two vamps, a male with long blond hair that hung down into my face. He was the one that attacked me at Richards's house.

"Haven't you heard of a ponytail?" I said and threw some of my power at him. He flew into the air, his hands reaching in vain to grab my arms as he soared twenty feet into the air. I scrambled out of the way before he struck the ground with a heavy thud.

I stood up and glanced around. Brigid still wrestled with the big vamp. Oni was in Aikido mode, holding off Angel while looking for an opportunity to use his stake.

My recent attacker had risen to his knees, shaking his head to clear his mind after the impact. I leaped into the air, landing with my knees on his back. He fell flat onto the ground, his nose snapping as it struck the hard dirt. I raised the stake above my head and jammed it down with all my strength into his back, behind his heart.

With a shriek, the vampire went rigid. Then its skin transformed, growing suddenly dry and desiccated, like a mummy.

The loud crash of rocks tumbling to the ground made me whirl around. The rock wall Isabella had been trapped against had fallen into dust, causing my Force Net to disintegrate.

The beautiful monster stepped over the rubble, glaring at me with a malevolence I had never seen before.

"You could have joined us," she said. "You could have been immortal!"

I rose, facing my foe. "Everyone dies, Isabella. You gave up living in order to prevent death."

"But I *am* alive! You sorcerers have it all wrong. Vampires aren't the living dead. Our bodies live, *we* live."

"The fossil behind me begs to differ," I said. I needed to keep her talking. I had no idea what spell to cast, but I had to think of one before she chose to attack.

Isabella shook her head slowly, her brow furrowed. "Why did you let that human," she motioned toward Mark, who was still doing as he was told and trying to force his way through the barrier over the hole, "beat you, when you could have killed him with a word?"

My sword! I had forgotten about it, but it was exactly what I needed. I paused to summon the blade. It would be visible to the world as it flew in a near straight line down my street and across the water to me, but I had to take the risk. With only a second or two of concentration, I called to it and felt the rush of magical energy surge from me, covering the distance to my home in a heartbeat. It found the sword where it hung on my wall and flew out my window. It was a simple spell, and cost me little. And I no longer needed to concentrate on it.

"I thought you'd know the answer," I said, trying to prolong the conversation. If I was lucky, my sword would arrive before she attacked. If I was *really* lucky, the sun would break through the fog and she would burn.

"I'm not a monster," I continued.

That was the wrong thing to say. Oh, it was witty—terribly witty—but it was also insulting, and I wasn't ready to insult her yet.

All curiosity vanished from her face as a wave of hatred consumed her. With a shriek of rage, she launched herself at me. One second she stood there, tense but gloating, the next she was on top of me. I fell under her charging force. I landed on the hard ground, and my head whipped backward, striking a rock.

There was a flash of light before my eyes, then everything went black.

Chapter Twenty-One

Laughter. Sick, terrible, maniacal laughter penetrated the darkness. Dim light seeped back into my consciousness. As my vision fought to regain focus, I was keenly aware of a sharp pain in the back of my head and a splitting headache.

Isabella hunched over me, her beautiful face inches from mine. I noticed the needle-like fangs that had grown outward in preparation for the death blow she meant to take. I wondered, as my mind returned to its normal clarity, how she could do that without making her whole face turn bat-like.

"You are a remarkable young man," she said, malice dripping like poison from every word. "But you're flawed. Your love of humanity, your compassion, makes you weak. Predators will always rule, will always thrive, because they don't care if their food is happy."

I tried to move, to force her off me, but she had her full weight on my body. Though I squirmed and pushed, I lacked the strength to dislodge her.

"You will die now, and the spell you placed on my hole will vanish and I will live to hunt again. Your death will be in vain, but at least I will get to feed—"

Her rant was interrupted when Brigid pulled hard on the vampire's luscious, black hair.

"Oh, *shut up*, will you?" Brigid said.

Isabella twisted and threw herself at Brigid, and the two tore at each other viciously. But the vampire leader had one last thing to say before she put all her focus on killing my dhampir friend.

"Mark, *kill him!*"

I climbed to my feet. My legs shook underneath me and the world spun as the injury to my head took its toll. Mark dropped the unconscious body of his friend and stalked toward me.

"You don't have to fight me," I said to him as he advanced, his hands held before him in the fists I was so familiar with. "You don't have to be her slave." I stumbled backward. Oni's vampire leaped on him, and they fell to the ground, struggling over a stake. Things had gone bad for him, but I couldn't help with Mark advancing on me.

I knew I had to defend myself from the bully, as he continued to stalk toward me, but I kept glancing at Oni. Angel had taken his stake and tossed it aside. Oni was out of options.

With a wave of my arm, like a lion tamer cracking his whip, I sent a line of energy at Oni's foe. It wrapped around the vampire's waist, and I yanked with all my might. Of course, if it was up to my muscles to do the job, the monster wouldn't have moved and I probably would have fallen on my face. But this was a spell, and what I lacked in physical strength, I made up for in the mystical. Angel was ripped from Oni with a shriek of anger and surprise and flew into my oncoming opponent. Mark toppled onto the vampire, and the two struggled to extricate themselves. I let go of the spell and ran toward Brigid and Isabella, skidding to a stop, my jaw agape.

Brigid lay motionless among the rubble of the old fort, her form covered in dirt and blood. Isabella stood facing me, a look of satisfaction on her face. At that moment, her face, although still as human-looking as ever, was no longer beautiful. The evil reflected in her smile and her eyes forever tainted the woman in my mind. There was no way I could ever be attracted to her again.

"It's your turn," she said, her voice husky, the joy of killing clear in her tone. She stepped toward me, and I gulped. The battle had taken too long and had drained most of my power. As capable as I was at magic, I was still only fifteen, and my energy reserves were less than optimal. As Isabella advanced on me, I knew I had no magic left in me to combat her. Brigid couldn't help. I could hear Oni once again battling his foe. It was me and her, and she looked strong and powerful.

"You could have made me strong," I said, desperation forcing me to delay the inevitable.

"That time is gone, boy." She grinned, and those needle-thin fangs glinted in the gathering dawn. They were clean of blood. She hadn't bitten Brigid. Relief surged through me, sending my blood rushing in my veins. It invigorated me.

I smiled. "But as strong as you are, you will never be happy. You will never be content. You will always hunger, and you will never be sated."

"It's true I live for the hunt. But I *relish* it. I don't need love or companionship when I have killing and blood." She stepped toward me and tensed for the spring I knew was about to come.

"Then why did you try to turn me? You wanted me to be one of you. You didn't want to kill me." A chill breeze blew in from the ocean behind me, parting the mist that had been burning off throughout the fight. I saw something in the air far away behind Isabella, like a curious bird, flying this way.

"I wanted someone to talk to. You have no idea how *boring* it is talking to them. I needed a man with intelligence and youthful vigor. But I didn't need you. I'll be just as happy feasting on your life essence. I bet a sorcerer will be a delicious treat!"

The strange bird was closer now, and I realized then it was no bird. I frowned. What was it?

"Now, the sun is rising, and I must go. You will die so I can return to my lair. Farewell, sweet boy."

I grinned at Isabella then. Not a smile of grim determination, nor one of maddening desperation. I beamed at the monster with humor mingled with relief. She frowned at this, then charged toward me . . .

. . . as my noble's rapier slid hilt-first into my hand.

I knelt quickly, my left leg extending straight behind me, my left hand on the ground for balance, in a perfect Passata Sotto maneuver. The thin rapier's blade slid neatly into my opponent's chest, even as she lunged at me. Her eyes went wide, her body rigid. I held that position as she transformed before me, no longer a beautiful young woman. She became like the others—a dry, disgusting hulk. I yanked my blade free and rose.

In the chaos of battle, I had forgotten the summoning. When most of my spells provided instant results, it was easy to overlook the one I had to wait for. Yet it hadn't forgotten, and it came. Out my window and down the street it had flown. It shot over the short stretch of water until at last it had come to its owner's aid.

Isabella fell to the ground and broke apart to blow away on the ocean wind like ashes from a fire.

I looked around wildly for my friends. Oni stood above Angel's desiccated form, a stake protruding from its chest. He was breathing heavy and had many cuts and abrasions, but he grinned at me then stomped on his dead foe. The vampire's body crumbled into dust.

I ran to Brigid, dropping the sword beside her. I felt desperately for a pulse. It was there. Faint, but there.

Oni knelt beside me. "Is she . . . ?"

I sighed. "She's alive. But she needs help."

Oni nodded and pulled out his phone.

Chapter Twenty-Two

"W-what happened?" It was Mark. He had snapped out of his vampire-induced trance, and now he was bewildered.

I looked up at Oni. "I have to get her to Aunt Elise. Can you deal with Mark?"

"Sure. You go. I've got this." He patted me on the shoulder, then went to Mark.

"How much do you remember?" he said to the bewildered kid as I took Brigid's hand and vanished.

We appeared in my room, Brigid lying on my bed with me beside it, my hand still clutching hers.

"Aunt Elise!" I called. "Hurry!"

I heard feet running up the stairs. My aunt burst into the room, her face twisted in concern, tears streaming down her cheeks. I stood up and ran to her. She pulled me into a tight hug and wouldn't let go for at least a minute.

"Please," I said, bringing her to her senses. "It's Brigid."

She let go of me, looked me over quickly, then, satisfied,

strode swiftly to the bedside.

"She's alive," Aunt Elise said grimly as she examined her. "But only just."

My aunt then switched into doctor mode and began giving me orders. We pulled the bed into the center of the room and she instructed me to cast a circle.

She had various potions brewing on the stove downstairs, and she told me to bring some of these up, along with a pot of water, a towel, and bandages. Then, she sent me away so that she could work.

I couldn't stand doing nothing as I waited, so I called Oni. He was still on the island.

"How are you?" I asked as soon as Oni answered. "Are you okay?"

He laughed. "I'm fine. Only a bunch of bruises and a few cuts. She never bit me, thanks to you. You saved my life back there."

"But you did great! A human kid fighting monsters like the best of us. Awesome!"

"Well, you know. I'm a cut above the rest."

I laughed. "How's Mark?"

"He's okay. He remembers some of it. Unfortunately, he remembers doing the bad things, but understands he was under someone else's control. He thinks it was hypnosis." Oni chuckled at that. "The others are coming around, and Mark's helping. Nobody seems badly hurt, although some of the vampires' slaves seem sick, like drug addicts in rehab."

"There's nothing we can do for them. Make them comfortable, and be nice to them."

"Okay. Mark says the nest is empty, but there's a lot of—

stuff—down there, if you know what I mean." Bodies. I knew. "The guards that Mark's gang beat up are coming around, and they seem to be free of the vamps' control now. And Jake and the others are fine. Mark's seeing to them. Should we call 911 about the pit? I think the victims' relatives would want to know."

I thought about that. Would the circumstances of their deaths make humans know vampires exist? I know the Alliance would want to keep that quiet.

"We should get the bodies to their families," Oni said to me as I debated with myself.

He was right. "Oni, how would the human authorities react to bodies that are drained of blood with pinprick holes in their skin? What conclusions would they draw?"

Oni pondered that before answering. "Well, the truth is, they wouldn't make the leap to vampires. We like to stay stupid about that stuff. They'll think it's a vampire cult. You know, humans that believe they're vampires, and ritualistically do that to their victims. They'll believe it was humans all along."

"Okay then. Call 911. You'll need a story to explain why you were there. Oh, and what about the vampires? Are their bodies still around?"

"Nope. They didn't stay mummified for long. They kind of crumbled up in the wind. You were right. They weren't human anymore."

"Good. All the supernatural evidence is gone. It's safe to call them."

I hung up.

Aunt Elise came downstairs an hour later. She looked tired, but smiled as she came to me.

"She'll be all right. I cured several of her smaller injuries, and the big ones are no longer serious. She'll need to rest for some time. I'm afraid you'll need to sleep in the guest room for the time being."

I slumped into my computer chair, relieved. Then, when she walked away from the bedside, I ran over and hugged her. I didn't let go for long time. I was tired, supremely tired, and part of me wanted to cry on her shoulder, but I held it back. I let go and took a seat. Now that I had a chance to relax, all the pains from the battle flooded me, and I put my head on the table, buried in my arms. The back of my head throbbed, and the headache still haunted me. And I was now aware of other bruises and cuts I had acquired during the fight.

Fingers began to gently probe the injury on the back of my head. Aunt Elise crossed to the sink, and I heard water running. She returned and carefully dabbed the injury with a cloth.

"You didn't say you got hurt," she said.

"I think only Oni got away without any damage."

"So, he's okay?"

"Yeah."

"And the pack?"

"Destroyed. Every last one of them."

Aunt Elise laid the cloth on my head. "And the slaves?"

"They woke up. They remember a little, but not much. I had Oni call the authorities."

Aunt Elise gasped. "You *did?*" I looked up at her disapproving tone, and she shook her head. "That's not what the Alliance would want."

"Oni said no one would believe it's vampires. They'll think it's a weird human cult."

"I hope so," was all she said.

Days passed, and life slowly went back to normal. Oni had only gotten a few cuts and bruises, plus a sprained knee. He had to wear a cast for a few weeks, but he treated it like a badge of honor. He deserved a *real* badge for his courage.

Mark recovered fully. The narcotic properties of the vampire bites wore off, and he was more of his old self within a handful of days. He was quieter than usual, and took to having occasional fits of melancholy, but all in all, he did fine.

Brigid took the longest to recover. It turned out dhampirs didn't have the advanced recuperative powers that vampires had, and her injuries nearly killed her. She stayed at our house for two weeks, moving to the guest room after the first few days, and Aunt Elise took good care of her.

I spent a lot of time with Brigid, talking about school and normal things. She didn't seem to want to discuss the battle. She understood that the vampires were destroyed, and that was all that mattered to her.

"You never told me how the dance went," she asked one day as I sat by her bed.

"Mark showed up in slave-mode and fought me, so it was a disaster."

"But what about your friends? Did you have fun before that happened?"

I thought back to that night and my time with Tracy. I nodded. "I think I did."

She flashed me a warm smile. "Good. And you didn't kiss any girls, right?"

"Of course not." I was lucky to say that with a clear conscience. Even though it had been touch and go for a moment.

"You're a gallant man, Malcus. One of a kind. And we have a connection. I'd be a fool to let you go."

I smiled. I was glad she said that.

That evening, I sat at my computer doing homework. I found it difficult to focus on schoolwork after the events on the island, but my teachers kept assigning it as though nothing had happened. For them, nothing had.

On a whim I navigated to *A Sorcerer's Guide to Magic, Monsters, & the Mythic World* to see if there was any news regarding my parents.

The page came up, and the usual headline slide show appeared. *Goblins spotted in Lithuania. Local family traumatized.* I smiled. I guess nothing big happens every day. The slide changed, and I froze, my eyes glued to the screen. The headline read in big, red letters:

Vampire nest cleared in a small New Hampshire town. Master vampire Isabella Kozlov destroyed in the raid.

I clicked on the link and it took me to the following article:

A raid occurred on a long-standing vampire nest located on an island off the coast of New Hampshire. The nest was the home of the infamous Isabella Kozlov, the fifty-year-old vampire who killed many prominent Russian diplomats before fleeing that country. The raid was executed by a single sorcerer, whose name has been withheld for security reasons, and was accompanied by a human and a friendly monster. All those who executed the raid are expected to survive, but the nest was completely wiped out. The Association is sending someone to take care of the pack's slaves and the handful of witnesses.

Our deepest thanks go out to the tireless sorcerer who undertook such a dangerous job and rid the world of one of the worst vampires in modern history.

I sat back in my chair, the words of the article turning circles in my mind. *How did they know? How* could *they know?*

One thing was certain, however: I had to uncover the mystery of this website and find out who was running it. I vowed to learn all there was to know about *A Sorcerer's Guide to Magic, Monsters, & the Mythic World.*

About the Author

Brad Younie writes books mostly about magic in the real world because he thinks people need a little excitement in their lives. Being an eternal teenager in a man's body, he owns a collection of swords (which he plays with), wands (which he plays with), and spends way too much time studying these things. A man with many hobbies, he plays guitar, reads books, watches movies, and fences with lightsabers and swords that are a bit sharper. But most of all, he weaves tales of magic and mystery that chills to the bone as it makes the heart race.

Visit www.bradyounie.com to learn more about his books.